Love & LIBATIONS

by patricia d. eddy

Love and Libations

Published February 2015

Editing & Interior Layout: Clare C. Marshall
Cover Design: Melody Barber

chapter one

"ONE MANHATTAN, COMIN' right up." Garrett James snagged the bottle of rye whiskey and upended it over the ice-filled cocktail shaker. A commotion shook the other end of the bar, drawing his attention. Danny Brogan was at it again. The man was a lousy drunk. Thirty-something, thin, but with a gut that said he preferred beer to the gym, the man had been here at Shade's Whiskey Station at the edge of Seattle's Columbia City neighborhood every night this week.

"Gimme the damn botthle," he slurred to Shade's part-time bartender and full-time bouncer, Rick.

"No. You're cut off. Call your lady and get her down here to pick you up."

"I can drive m'self."

"Like hell you can. Tell you what. If you can manage to stack these three shot glasses one on top of another, I'll let you walk out of here. Otherwise, it's your lady or the cops. But someone's coming to get you." Rick was six-foot-three-inches of solid muscle, a former marine, and the toughest son of a bitch Garrett had ever met.

"Fucking prick," Danny spat when the second glass fell out of his hand and rolled along the bar.

Garrett turned back to his customer and strained the Manhattan into a glass, added two rye-soaked cherries on a plastic toothpick, and flashed his smile. "There you go, ma'am. That'll be ten dollars."

"Start a tab, handsome," the brunette replied. "And it's *miss*." A not-so-subtle wave of her left hand revealed no ring. She was gorgeous, but in a plastic, perfectly sculpted way that said she'd spent more time under the knife than anywhere else. Her credit card proclaimed her one Mitzi May and Garrett fought not to scowl. Most of the time he loved his job. He was a people person, preferring the bar to an office, stuck at a desk all day. Although Shade's was one of the better bars in the neighborhood, it still got its fair share of drunks, along with women who were destined to be cougars. Mitzi didn't look much over thirty, but for all Garrett could tell, beneath that plastic surgery, she could have been sixty.

"Will do, miss." He turned and ambled off towards the cash register, his left leg throbbing a little under his prosthetic. Absently, he rubbed it, only then realizing that the real pain was below mid-thigh—where the prosthetic took over. *Dammit.* He hadn't had a bout of phantom pain in a few months, but this one stabbed him deep.

He braced his hands against the counter, watching Danny out of the corner of his eye. The man was slumped over the bar with a cell phone clutched in his hand.

"Get down here," Danny slurred. "I need a ride." A few seconds passed and the drunk's eyes narrowed. "I don't care what you're doing, get the fuck down here, now." He threw the phone on the counter, where it knocked over another customer's whiskey.

"Hey, watch it!" Garrett stalked over, wiped up the

spilled liquor, and poured the customer another. "This is a bar, not your own personal trash bin."

"Fuck you."

"Original."

Danny's shot glass sailed towards Garrett's head and Garrett ducked, his hand shooting up to grab the glass before it shattered. "Rick, take him in back. Now."

Rick lumbered over and grabbed Danny by the arm. The bouncer hauled the intolerable drunk off the barstool and into the small office Shade kept for the few hours a week he spent in the bar. It was largely empty, not even a computer, so Danny couldn't do much damage in there. Rick would stay with him until whoever he called showed up.

Six beers, two whiskey sours, and a cosmo (who the hell came here to order a cosmo?) later, the door opened. Silhouetted in the street light, a tall, curvaceous vision swiveled her head from side to side, possibly wondering if this was truly a place she wanted to be.

"Help you, ma'am?" Garrett called out, making his way to the side of the bar closest to the door so he could see her better.

She stepped inside, shoulders hunched, lower lip trapped askew beneath her teeth. Bathed in the dim bar lights, she was every bit as lovely as he'd imagined when the backlight had transformed her, momentarily, into an angel. A black trench coat couldn't hide the curve of her hips or swell of her breasts. She had long, reddish-blond hair, pulled up into a ponytail. Her cheeks were flushed from the chill of the night air, or maybe that was from something else, the discomfort of a dozen pairs of eyes on her? Moss-green eyes flicked around, and when her gaze settled on him, he found an intensity there that was both curious and a bit uncomfortable.

"I got a call. My . . . uh . . . boyfriend is drunk. I think this is his place." Her gentle voice belied the fear, sadness, and disgust in her expression. Her arms tightened around her body, and her fingers trembled before she clenched her hands into fists.

"Danny Brogan?"

"Y-yes."

"He's in back. I'll get him for you. Have a seat." Garrett motioned to one of the bar stools, but Danny's girlfriend didn't move. "Sit, darlin'. You look like you're about to fall over." He filled a glass of water from the fountain and slid it towards her. "Are you sure you want to leave with him?" Garrett didn't know why he asked her that, or why he suddenly had a vision of her cowering from the drunk, but he wanted the lady to relax. Even for a minute. Maybe smile.

"I'll be fine. I know how to handle him," she said, her gaze hardening. "Who has his keys?"

"That'd be my bouncer. You need to leave his car here?"

The water remained untouched in front of her.

"No. I don't have a car. I'll drive him home."

He took another good look at her. The flushed cheeks, the light sparkle of sweat on her temple, the reddened skin on her hands. "Did you walk?"

"Bus. Not that it's any of your business. Can I have my boyfriend, please? I'd like to get home."

"Fine." Garrett loped towards the back. "Rick! Bring Mr. Brogan out here. His girlfriend wants to take him home."

Rick walked Danny out with a firm grip on his bicep. The drunk stumbled, but Rick held him up and half-dragged him to the front door where the redhead stood, shifting from foot to foot.

"Come on, man, onemoredrink," Danny slurred, trying to reach the bar.

"Danny, it's time to go home."

"Shut up, Lilah. Didn't anyone ever tell you not to come between a man and his liquor?"

Lilah flinched, took a step back, and tried to school her face into a mask. Garrett's anger got the better of him. He came out from behind the bar and took his position in front of Lilah.

"That's no way to talk to your girlfriend."

Lilah grabbed Garrett's arm. "It's fine. Please. Give me his keys. We'll get out of your hair." Her gaze pleaded with him, as did the insistent grip on his arm.

Garrett jerked his head towards the door. "Get that shitshow out of here," he said, hoping Rick would understand that Garrett wanted a moment alone with Lilah. He did, and dragged Danny outside.

"He doesn't mean to be an ass," Lilah whispered. "He hasn't been sleeping well. His job is really stressful . . . "

"That's no excuse. Lilah?" She nodded. "I don't care what's going on in his life. You don't disrespect your girlfriend like that. He's got both his legs. A job. A beautiful woman willing to take the bus down here to pick his sorry ass up."

She blushed, clutching her purse to her body. "He's not a bad guy. Not really. Does he owe any money?"

"No. I know the type. I made him pay cash."

A laugh bubbled up, but she clapped a hand over her mouth. The light in her eyes danced for all of a minute before it died and she nodded. "Well, thank you."

"Lilah?"

She turned back, her hand on the door. "Yes?"

"Lilah what?"

"McKinney."

"Good luck with him, Lilah McKinney."

With a frown, the angel walked out the door.

~

Weak rays of sunlight peeked through her drapes. Lilah rolled over, shocked to find the bed empty. "Danny?"

The night rushed back to her. She'd driven Danny home, enduring his drunken ramblings the entire way. She hated to drive, largely because she was so bad at it—at least that's what he'd told her over and over again. "You're going to get yourself killed, Lilah. Can't you manage to go over the speed limit?"

When they'd gotten back to their Southcenter apartment, she'd tried to help him into bed, but he'd shoved her away once they'd reached the living room and he'd poured himself another drink moments later. She'd gone to bed alone, and by all accounts, he'd slept on the couch.

"Danny?" Lilah shrugged into her robe and belted it tightly around her flannel pajamas as she left the bedroom. She needed coffee.

The living room was Danny-free. His keys weren't where he'd dropped them and his jacket was gone. The blanket she'd left for him was still folded on the back of the couch.

"Shit!" A sharp pain stabbed through the bottom of her left foot. Glass. "What the hell?" The bourbon bottle. He'd probably thrown it against the wall when he'd emptied it. She refused to buy him alcohol. Her one and only little rebellion. *Well, not the only one, just the only one he knows about.* He'd probably gone to the store for more bourbon. But based on how little had been left when they'd gotten home, that had to have been hours ago. Where was he?

Lilah limped into the bathroom and examined the ball of her foot. A shard of glass the size of her pinky stuck out of the tender flesh. She plucked it out, staunched the blood with one of the blue hand towels, and wondered how long this peace would last. Was he drunk in his car somewhere? Passed out along the side of the road? Or had he gotten into an accident? Killed someone, or himself?

"Please, not someone else," she whispered. A sob welled up in her throat. When had she gotten so low that all she cared about was him not hurting others? *You should love your partner,* she thought. Vague memories of their first few months together swirled in her mind. Had she ever loved him? The pregnancy had locked them together. Once that was no longer a factor, she should have left, but he took care of her. Nursed her back to health. She owed him. Everything.

She sank down to the bathroom floor, tears gathering in her eyes. This was no way to live. Her part-time job at the library didn't pay her enough to leave. Hell, she barely made enough to pay her half of the rent and keep ten dollars a week for her Friday latte and scone splurge. She didn't have any other skills. Not according to Danny. Her design work was shit, her writing was shit, and she hadn't used her business degree in six years.

The ringing phone elicited a yelp. "Shit." She limped out to the kitchen and picked up the land line. "Hello?"

"Lilah McKinney?"

"Y-yes. Who's calling?"

"Seattle Police, ma'am. Officer Harrison. We've got a Danny Brogan in custody. Booked on a DUI. He's sleeping it off, but his blood alcohol came back at point-one-two. We've taken his license. He woke up enough an hour ago to give us your name and number, then told us not to call you before nine. Something about you needing your beauty sleep."

Lilah snorted. Yes, that sounded like Danny. "Did he hurt anyone?"

"No, ma'am. He ended up half in a ditch off of Alki, took out a street lamp and two park benches, but luckily he didn't hit anyone."

Relief had her sinking back against the counter. "What do I do? About Danny?"

"He'll be arraigned in a couple of hours. If you showed up around two, that would be fine. He'll get a court date sometime next month. Until then, no driving and no drinking."

Good luck with that, she thought. "Do I ask for you?"

"Yes, ma'am. Five hundred, Fifth Avenue."

"If I show up, will I be able to get his car? I have a valid license. A spare set of keys."

"You'll have to pay to get it out of impound. Are you on the registration?"

"No." Her name wasn't on anything. Not the lease, not the car, not even her computer's warranty.

"Then you'll need some proof of ownership," Officer Harrison said.

"I'll see what I can do. Thank you, officer."

A few hours later, with the car's pink slip in her purse,

she boarded the bus for the jail. It took her an hour and two transfers. The rain hadn't let up all morning and her shoes were soaked through by the time she arrived and met with Officer Harrison, a soft, kindly man with bushy blond eyebrows. The officer gave her a stack of paperwork to fill out, Danny's personal effects, and went to retrieve him.

"Danny, are you okay?" She rushed up to him, holding her breath at the stink of vomit, sweat, and bourbon. Still, she threw her arms around him. Danny rested his stubbly cheek on her shoulder.

"I'm sorry, baby. I was stupid."

"Shh. We're going to go home now. Well, once we get your car."

Between the paperwork for retrieving the car and the DUI, it was after dark when they got home. Danny had been relatively silent the entire day, occasionally holding her hand or brushing his fingers against her thigh while she drove. He was almost tender. When she steered him into the shower and told him that she'd make him dinner, he kissed her cheek. "I don't know what I'd do without you, baby."

"Clean up, Danny. We'll watch a movie tonight."

"I don't deserve you."

No, you don't. "We deserve each other." She couldn't bring herself to use any term of endearment. She didn't love him. He was all she had. All she could expect.

She'd almost escaped the bathroom when he grabbed her and dragged her into the shower with him. "Danny, no. I don't want to get wet."

"Too late." The shower spurted on and drenched her in icy water.

"It's not even hot yet!"

He turned her so she was facing away from him, pulled down her yoga pants and panties, and bent her over. The water streamed down her cheeks, getting into her eyes. She hated this. Hated that the only time he paid any attention to her was when he didn't have to look at her. His fingers probed inside her, the shower water her only lubrication before his dick slammed into her. She shivered, the water taking its own sweet time to come up to temperature. With a grunt, Danny thrust hard, his hands on her hips making sure she wouldn't fall.

Lilah closed her eyes, letting him get his rocks off. "Oh God, baby. God," he panted. A final spasm and he came, pulling out and slapping her ass. She reached for the soap, cleaned herself off, and stripped the rest of the way, leaving her soaking wet sweatshirt, pants, and underwear in the corner of the shower. She'd clean them up later. It wasn't like he did any housework. That was her job.

Once in their bedroom, she stared at her naked body in the full length mirror on the back of the door. She hated it—hated seeing what she looked like, but Danny needed it, so it stayed.

The three scars crisscrossed her belly in jagged pinkish lines. Her hands covered the slight swell to her abdomen, a single tear spilling out of the corner of her right eye. The baby—a girl—had been twenty weeks. The size of a banana. But she'd loved her all the same. The attack had ruined everything. Her child, her relationship, everything.

"Baby? Get me a beer!"

Everything.

Danny was almost sweet the next day. He made a pot of coffee, filling a travel mug for her before they left the apartment. "I'm sorry you have to take me to work, baby."

"It's okay, Danny. Call me when you're ready to leave and I'll pick you up. I know how you hate taking the bus."

She dropped him off at his office downtown and took Highway 99 up to the Lake Forest Park Library. She loved it up here. The patrons were all sweet and respectful and her supervisor, Halley, was fair and encouraging.

"Hey, Lilah. I need you to work the Information Desk today."

"Gotcha." She paused before heading off. She had to ask. "Halley, is there any chance I could pick up a few more hours?"

Lilah's supervisor set her coffee mug down, turning her blue-eyed gaze to the floor. "I'm sorry, sweetie. The budget is stretched thin. I can barely pay you for the eighteen hours a week you work now."

"Oh. Okay." She turned, trying not to let her voice reflect her disappointment. "Thanks."

At the end of her shift, Halley caught her in the break room. "I made a couple of calls. This isn't public knowledge yet, but the Green Lake branch is losing their personnel director at the end of the month. I recommended you for the position and if you want it, it's basically yours. You'll need to complete the application, but Janice, the current director, trusts my recommendation. It's full time, forty hours a week."

Lilah's heart sank. Danny would never agree to her working full time. He wanted her home, cooking dinner for him every night, cleaning up his messes, dependent on him. She'd hoped for another five or six hours a week, not twenty-two. "Um, I don't know. I don't think I can handle full time." She refilled her travel mug with coffee and stared down at her feet. "I need to move at the end of the year and I can't do that on my current salary, but he—" She stopped and shook her head. She'd been about to confess that Danny wouldn't let her take the job. Panic gripped her and she took a step back.

"Where are you moving?" Halley popped the top on a can of Coke.

"I don't know. But I can't leave without a few months' rent saved up. Right now, I don't have any cushion." *Why am I admitting all this?* The answer came quickly. *Because you don't have anyone to talk to and Halley asked.*

"Leave? Oh thank God." Halley leaned forward and took Lilah's hand. "No one deserves to be miserable all the time."

Lilah twisted her hand away. "Move. I meant move. Leave Southcenter. Somewhere closer." The words tumbled out too quickly, but she couldn't stop them.

"Lilah, if you need help getting out . . . "

"I have to go." She raced out of the break room, out of the building, and hid in Danny's car. She clutched the steering wheel with white-knuckled fingers. She'd come dangerously close to confessing everything. Danny's temper, his constant berating, his DUI. She hadn't had a close friend in years. She and Halley chatted for a few minutes in the mornings, but Lilah always kept things light. She went to the movies or to lunch with Pamela once in a while, but she'd given up inviting her over to the apartment after Danny had gotten drunk and come on to the poor woman. Pam called every week and they made small talk for an hour, but that was as close to a friend as she'd ever have unless she left him. He drove everyone away with his rude, obnoxious, or controlling behavior.

When she pulled alongside Rainier Tower in downtown Seattle, Danny was waiting outside. "About time, Li."

"I hate that name, you know that."

"Dammit. I don't want to fight. It was a long day. Take me home. What's for dinner?"

"Spaghetti."

"Again? Can't you cook anything else?" His whiny tone grated on her nerves.

"I *can*, but you haven't given me grocery money this week. Spaghetti is all we have. If you want me to go to the store, then give me some cash and I'll make you anything you want." She turned onto Interstate 5, heading for Southcenter. They lived forty minutes out of downtown, mainly because Danny preferred to drink a significant portion of his income these days. They'd had to move from their Sand Point apartment two years ago, after the consulting firm he worked for lost a big client and profits fell dramatically. That was the point where his drinking had gone from occasional to frequent and his behavior had taken a turn for the worse.

"I didn't go to the bank today. I'll deal with that shit tomorrow. Spaghetti is fine."

Lilah mustered her courage and cleared her throat. "Um, Danny?"

"Yeah?"

"I'm up for a promotion at work. It'd be full time at the Green Lake branch. Supervising. I really want it. I think I'd be good at it. We could have more of a cushion. Maybe go on a little vacation this summer."

"You'd be crap at managing people, Li."

The words stung. Her grip on the steering wheel tightened so she wouldn't start to cry. "How do you know? Maybe I'd be good at it. I filled in for Halley the week of Christmas. I loved it."

"You just want to be better than me, don't you?" He slammed his hand against the passenger door. "Nothing's ever good enough for you. Not me, not your job, not our apartment. Nothing. I give you a good life. Hell, I gave you the best years of *my* life and now you want to trade up. There's probably a hot young guy working at Green Lake, isn't there?"

Her denial was a little too slow.

"There is. *That's* what this is all about. Don't expect me to make it easy for you to have an affair. If you take that job, we're through. You can move out. You'll fuck another man over my dead body."

"Danny, please. All I want is to have something of my own. Something I'm good at. Can't you see that? I don't want to leave," she said, unsure whether she was lying or telling the truth. She didn't know. She didn't know anything anymore.

"Turn here. I need to stop at the liquor store."

"No. You're not supposed to drink. The DUI."

"Fuck it. Anyone would drink after this conversation. Now, Lilah. Or you'll be sorry."

She was already sorry.

~

"Garrett, stick to the menu," Shade said, slamming his fist on the bar. "We don't serve custom drinks here."

The techno music Shade had chosen for the night grated along Garrett's spine. He hated the days the owner came in. Shade watched him and Rick like a hawk, ensuring their pours were shy, their tickets were punched perfectly, and that any desire for an inventive cocktail was met with a "We don't do that here." One of Garrett's regulars, a thirty-something businessman named Harv, had asked for something warming with bourbon and Garrett ached to flex his creative muscles. He had this idea for a drink with bourbon, muddled lemons, and honey. Kind of like the throat tonic his dad had given him when he was a kid. He'd toss in cinnamon and cloves if the bar stocked them, but it didn't. Hell, the place barely served food. The kitchen was limited to greasy chicken nuggets that weren't even up to McDonald's standards, nachos with fake cheese sauce, and frozen pizzas re-heated in the microwave.

"Yessir." He saluted Shade, snapping to attention with a grimace. Shade knew Garrett was former military, but the closest Shade had come to serving was seeing the Humvees heading down Interstate 5 to Joint Base Lewis-McChord.

"That's the spirit," Shade said with a smile.

Stupid fuck has no idea I'm mocking him. Garrett turned back to the bottles of liquors and mixers and made the standard hot toddy, the only hot drink Shade allowed. He slid it in front of Harv. "Sorry, man. You heard the boss." He lowered his voice. "Come back tomorrow and I'll have something for you I think you'll like."

Harv grinned and handed Garrett a twenty dollar bill. "Keep the change, Garrett."

"Dude, the drink was only six bucks."

Shrugging, Harv took a sip of his hot toddy. "Consider it an investment. When you get your own place, I expect something awesome on the menu."

"Yessir." This salute was genuine, and not only because Garrett liked Harv. The man was a former marine. They'd often talk shop—or what used to be shop—on slow nights. Harv never saw hard combat, but he served around the same time Garrett had, ten years ago. While Garrett had only lasted two years before the attack had taken his leg, Harv served for five, rising to the rank of sergeant major.

"Any progress on that front?"

Garrett looked around. Shade had disappeared into the back room. "I'm goin' to the bank to see about a loan in a few days. Got a partner—former army buddy—and we're hopeful."

"Where you looking?" Harv took another sip, cupping his hands around the hot mug.

"Everywhere. I'd love Green Lake or Roosevelt. There's too much competition in Ballard and the prices are through the roof. As long as I'm out of this shithole, I don't really care." Garrett leaned back against the bar, his gaze scanning the room. There were at most two dozen patrons tonight. Slow for a Thursday. "I've been here for five years. Helped turn this place around. And Shade still won't let me put a single custom drink on the menu."

"Well, good luck. You're too damn talented to be wasted in this place. Thanks for the drink."

Garrett couldn't shake Shade's scrutiny for the rest of the night. When the owner left, well after nine, the entire mood in the bar shifted along with the music.

~

Later that night, as Garrett wiped down the bar, his phone buzzed in his pocket. "Hey, Pop. What's up?"

"Your ma' wants to know when you're fixin' to visit."

Garrett chuckled. "It's the shittiest time of the year in Seattle. Don't tempt me with Hawaii."

"Why the hell not? Get your sorry ass out here for a week."

"You know I'm savin' every dime, Pop. And don't even think about sendin' me a ticket. Plus, Shade would probably fire my ass if I asked for a week off. Fucking prick."

"Good riddance."

"Yeah, I know. But until I get my own place, he pays well enough and my regulars are good tippers. Ed and I are goin' to the bank for a loan in a few days. If it comes through, I promise I'll take a few days between quittin' here and startin' the work on Libations. I miss Ma."

"And not your old Pop?"

"Nope. Not one bit." The two had gone back and forth like this for years. Two strong men, both army vets, neither willing to open up much. They had an understanding. These bits of banter were the equivalent of saying *I love you.* They'd only said the words once in the past ten years—the day Garrett had told his parents he was going to get fitted with his prosthetic and stop moping around in his wheelchair at their old house in Georgia. Two years he'd wasted: angry, afraid, and letting his body go to hell. His parents had moved to Hawaii soon after, once they'd known he was going to be okay.

They talked through the rest of Garrett's closing procedures: flipping the chairs up on the tables, shutting off the jukebox, putting the cash drawer in the safe, and locking up. Garrett climbed into his truck. "I gotta go, Pop. It's late and I'm wiped. I'll call Ma tomorrow."

"You'd better."

The drive back to his apartment only took ten minutes

this late at night. He climbed the stairs slowly, his leg aching a bit. He'd been working too much and hadn't been taking care of himself. At least he had the next day off.

Pausing at his mailbox, he grinned. Nomar came through, yet again. Garrett's former lieutenant fancied himself a bit of an artist and came up with a few different logo renditions for Libations—the name of the bar/restaurant that Garrett had dreamed of starting for years. He'd taken a job tending bar after he learned to function with his prosthetic, found he liked it, and had traded his dream of being a fireman for business ownership. He'd dreamt of protecting and saving people right up until the doctor in the army hospital informed him that his right leg would have to be amputated mid-thigh. At least if he was the boss, his hard work would mean something—or so he hoped. He could bring joy to people, even if he couldn't protect them.

Silence filled his apartment. He welcomed it after the night at Shade's. Or did he? He was thirty-two and he hadn't had a meaningful relationship in years. His last serious girlfriend hated his job. She couldn't understand that bartenders *had* to flirt with customers. It didn't mean anything. Smiling, joking, winking at his female clients (as well as the occasional gay male), were all part of the job. He'd never so much as looked twice at a pretty woman, other than the one he was with at the time, and he *never* touched them. Never even fantasized about them. Betty had walked out of Shade's after throwing her drink in his face.

Garrett dropped his pants and rubbed the top of his right thigh. He removed the outer sleeve he wore, loosened the mechanism that kept the prosthetic in place, gently removed it, and set it aside. Rolling down the compression sleeve that helped protect his stump, he sighed and rubbed at one of the deeper scars that ran towards his hip. It was a lot like taking off your shoes after a long day on your feet. He was lucky. His parents had taken out a loan to help him pay for the best prosthetic on the market—much better than the one his insurance wanted to cover. He rarely had trouble. Still, it felt good to be free of it, even though it meant he had to depend on his crutches.

Tucking them under his arms, he headed back out to the living room to unwind with a glass of scotch and some mindless TV.

chapter two

Fucking idiot. Garrett pulled himself up smoothly, again and again. Thirty-six reps later, he lowered himself carefully, putting his weight on his good leg first, then his prosthetic one. He'd have to cut his workout short because Shade couldn't schedule worth shit and needed him to come in on his day off. His tattooed arms shone with sweat. Wiping his face with a towel, he ambled over to the free weights. Curls, dips, and chest presses were next, followed by reverse crunches. He'd save the lower body workout for the next day. He'd run a few miles this morning and his leg was a little achy. Standing behind the bar for six hours wasn't his idea of a good time, especially tonight. But every extra shift brought him closer to his dreams.

Later, leaning against the wall of the shower, the water rinsed away his sweat. Suds ran down over the tree of life tattooed over his right ribs. The roses, the lightning, and the skulls on his arms, and the dragon that wound its way around his good leg, all the way down to his calf, glistened beneath the soap. He'd gone a little crazy with the ink after losing most of his right leg. Full arm sleeves, both pectorals, and his left leg. His hands were ink-free, as were his left foot, neck, and lower back.

But for a while, the pain of the tattoo needle helped him deal with the pain of his injuries. He didn't regret it. The tats were who he was, who he wanted to be. They were strength, beauty, and power.

Washing off the suds, he let his mind wander. His last date had been laughable. They'd gone for drinks down at Zig Zag, and he thought they'd been having a good time. But when she'd reached over to squeeze his thigh and had encountered the hard resin of his prosthesis, she'd recoiled. Hadn't even waited long enough to finish her drink. At least she'd apologized for being shallow and reactive. "I'm sorry. I shouldn't let it affect things, but it does. I've gotta go. See you around, Garrett."

See you around. Yeah. Right. Wendy was long gone. He palmed his cock, needing a release. It swelled in his grip, visions of a curvy redhead swirling behind his closed lids. He'd always had a thing for redheads.

A groan started deep in his gut, exploding as his balls tightened and his cock spasmed, shooting his load against the wall of the shower. Shit. Lilah. He'd been thinking of Lilah.

A week later, on Valentine's Day, Garrett was suffering through his sixth night in a row behind the bar when the door opened. The winter storm brought in a swirl of leaves, rain, and a man with a redhead tucked in the crook of his arm. Lilah. Garrett didn't even see Danny Brogan. His entire focus was on her. Her gaze flicked around the room, landing on him for an uncomfortable pause before her boyfriend released her. "Go sit at the bar, baby. I'm gonna hang with the boys."

"Danny. You're not supposed—"

"I'm not fucking driving. Give me a break. I need to let off some steam. Have a glass of wine or two." Danny dug out his credit card and shoved it into her hand. Without a backwards glance, he left her for a table of businessmen in the corner of the room who were on their second round of boilermakers.

Lilah glanced at Danny. A brief glimmer of sadness appeared in her eyes, but she blinked it away. She took a seat at the corner of the bar, as far away from him as she could, and withdrew an e-reader from her bag.

Garrett wiped down the bar and set a glass of water and a bowl of pretzels in front of her. "Lilah. A glass of wine?" He turned around, perusing the bottles on the shelf. "Wait. Let me guess. A French 75?"

Lilah snorted. "Maybe for brunch. Or if the only alternative is white wine. Knob Creek. Neat."

Holy shit. That's sexy as hell. He stuttered his acknowledgement, unable to keep the disbelief from his tone.

"Women can drink liquor too, you know. And if I'm going to drink, it's going to be the good stuff."

"Yes, ma'am." He poured her a double, punched in a single, and set the drink and the receipt down in front of her.

"Thanks, uh...?" She raised a reddish-blond brow.

"Garrett."

"Do you serve food?" She looked around the room, her gaze lingering on her boyfriend and his cronies before she shook her head and met Garrett's eyes once more.

"Nothin' that you'd want to eat. Why?"

"Because I'm probably going to be here half the night and I haven't had dinner yet. I had to drive him here right after work. So much for Valentine's Day."

"Had to?"

Lilah snorted again. It was the cutest little sound and Garrett tried to hide his smile behind a glass of water. "He lost his license. I'm his chauffeur for the next few . . . well . . . I don't know how long. His trial isn't for another month."

"DUI?"

She nodded.

"Can I ask you somethin'?"

Her pale green eyes narrowed. "If I say no, you're just going to ask anyway. I know your type. Nosy and all self-righteous. I bet you were in the military."

Garrett shrugged. "Army."

"Figures. So ask."

"Why are you with him?" He leaned on the bar, his bare forearms drawing her gaze.

"He takes care of me."

"He's left you alone, at a bar, while he drinks with his buddies. After a DUI. On Valentine's Day. That doesn't sound like he's all that responsible."

"Danny has his faults. We all do." She took a sip of her bourbon and her eyelids fluttered closed. "I'd like to be alone, please. If I have to sit here for the next few hours, I'd rather not spend the whole time defending Danny or my own choices."

He held up his hands. "You're the boss."

A last snort and Lilah returned her attention to her Kindle.

She'd finished her book and Danny was still drinking. She cursed his consulting firm and his coworkers, half of whom were around the table with him, drowning their sorrows. The firm had lost another big client, and everyone was stressed out. Danny had always been fond of alcohol, but the stress of losing business had turned him from a social and weekend drinker to a stupor-every-night drinker. She'd even suggested that he go to an AA meeting, but he'd screamed at her, locked her out of their bedroom, and not spoken to her for three days. *"I'm not a fucking addict, you stupid bitch. I work hard and I deserve to let loose when I get home."*

She cringed at the memory. If only she'd been brave enough to take that job Halley offered her. But she was too scared that Danny would find out and make good on his threats. She had no credit and no savings. If she wanted to leave, she was going to have to save up first.

"Here."

A wrapped, greasy cylinder resting on a paper plate slid into her field of vision.

"What's this?"

"A sandwich. I didn't know what you liked, but I got two. That one's a fried chicken club on sourdough. I got a Philly cheesesteak too if you'd rather that."

Lilah blushed and stammered. "Wh-where did you get this?"

"Food truck a few blocks away. They're good. I eat there once a week."

"I don't have any cash." She glanced over her shoulder at Danny. He'd reached the sloppy stage. If she wasn't careful, he'd get all the way to angry in another hour or so.

"My treat. I don't want you driving him home on a double and an empty stomach. But feel free to tip well. Deal?" Garrett unwrapped his sandwich and bit into the gooey mess.

Lilah tore into her own sandwich and her stomach growled. She'd already finished the bowl of pretzels and two glasses of water, but she needed this. The bourbon had gone to her head. The first bite elicited a groan. She leaned into the bar, the corners of her lips tugging upwards automatically. "Oh God. This is awesome."

A laugh shook his entire body and he set down his sandwich, swallowing hard. "I worried you'd be one of those women who picked at their food, askin' me for a knife and fork for that monstrosity."

"Hardly," she answered through a mouthful of chicken. Mayonnaise trailed down her hand and she dipped her head and licked it off, grinning at him.

Holy shit. That is about the hottest thing I've ever seen a woman do. Garrett couldn't tear his gaze away from Lilah's lips. She ate the sandwich with such gusto that he wondered if she'd lick the wrapper when she was done. He had to admit he'd pay to see that. They talked a little bit about her choice of reading material—thrillers and suspense mostly—though she said tonight's book had been non-fiction. He kept the conversation light, not wanting to upset her with more talk about Danny and her seemingly poor choice in boyfriends. She had an easy smile, though she kept glancing back at Danny—possibly to see if he noticed the two of them talking. Garrett did his best to keep busy a foot or so away from her, trying not to be obvious in his attentions. He was beginning to suspect what type of man Danny Brogan was, and it wasn't a good one.

Two hours passed in the blink of an eye, and Garrett

couldn't remember ever enjoying a Valentine's Day more. It was too bad there wouldn't be a kiss at the end of it. The only dark spot was Brogan. The man downed five beers and three shots of whiskey before Garrett cut him off, and then started getting his slightly-more-sober buddies to order the drinks for him. By the time Garrett caught on, the man could barely stand.

"Time to go, baby," Danny slurred, throwing his arm around Lilah's shoulders and half-dragging her off the chair.

"I have to pay the bill," she said firmly.

"I've seen you making eyes at my girl." Danny hardened his gaze at Garrett. "She's mine, asshole."

"I've been *talkin'* to her, Brogan. Like a human being. Which is more than I've seen you do tonight," Garrett spat, printing out the check. He handed it to Lilah.

"Gimme." Danny snatched the bill and the card out of her hand. He scrawled his name and tossed it back, not even bothering to leave a tip. "Get your ass in the car, Lilah."

"Hey, dickweed, shut the fuck up if you ever want to come back here. Rick? I think we're about to have a problem with this dipshit."

Danny ignored Garrett's warning. "Lilah, now."

Garrett came around the bar, drawing up to his full height. He had at least four inches on Danny Brogan and fifty pounds of muscle. Drinking every night wasn't the best fitness plan. With his brown-eyed gaze fixed on Lilah, he forced himself between the drunken mess and the misplaced angel. "Lilah, do you want to go with him?"

"Stay out of this, Garrett. It's none of your business. I'm fine."

He leaned in, lowering his voice. "I can call the cops."

Danny lunged and grabbed Garrett. The drunk spun him and threw him against the bar. A couple of pint glasses crashed to the floor, shattering. With a roar, Danny stuck his leg out and caught Garrett in the ankle. His prosthetic ankle. Before Garrett knew it, his ass hit the floor and Rick had Danny by the arms.

"Shit!" Lilah yelped, dropping down to one knee in front of Garrett. "Are you okay?"

She smelled like lilacs. *Lilacs for Lilah*. Garrett raised his gaze to meet hers. "Yeah." He rapped on his calf. The titanium limb with the resin overlay was built to withstand anything a normal person could possibly throw at it. Hell, he could hit it with a sledgehammer and probably not do more than scuff the custom paint job. A tug on the leg of his jeans revealed the silvery ankle joint.

"Oh." Her cheeks flamed red. The blush extended down to her chest and out to her ears. The simple, silver hoops dangled from lobes he desperately wanted to touch.

Shit. She was in a relationship. What the hell was he thinking? *That she's dating a slack-jawed pigfucker and deserves better.*

"Iraq," he offered in explanation. Grabbing above his knee, he gave a quick tug to ensure his leg hadn't come loose and accepted Lilah's hand to help him up. It was warm, soft, and stronger than he'd anticipated. Testing his weight, he nodded, satisfied the limb wasn't harmed. Lilah glared at her boyfriend, still held in Rick's iron grip.

"Well, now you've done it," she muttered, then clasped her hand over her mouth for a second. "I mean, crap. I need to get him home."

"He's not going home, ma'am," Rick said. "He attacked Garrett. He's going to the drunk tank for the night."

Wide eyes looked between the three men. "Please, don't."

"Lilah?" Garrett reached out a hand, stopping short of her arm. She nodded, and allowed him to guide her to a stool. A few patrons watched them, but no one interfered. At Shade's, drinkers minded their own business. "Are you in danger at home?"

"No."

"Lilah."

"No. I'm not. He's a mean drunk. Seriously. But he's never violent. I don't know what got into him tonight."

"I'm nearly a buck ninety, darlin'. And that leg is pretty damn solid. It takes a lot to knock me off my feet. If he turned a fraction of that anger on you, I'm afraid you wouldn't stand a chance." Garrett pressed the glass of water into her hands. She gulped half the liquid down, warily watching Danny slumped against the bar, Rick ready to spring at any sudden movement.

"I'm not as fragile as I look, Garrett."

"Didn't say you were."

"Please. Let me take him home. I'll make sure he comes back and apologizes—and doesn't drink—tomorrow. You'll be saving me a lot of grief."

There was something about that voice, the pleading look in her eyes, that softened Garrett's resolve. "Fine. Rick, help the lady with her . . . baggage."

"The fucktard needs to go to jail, Garrett."

"Not if he doesn't come back again. It's fine. But he's paying for the glasses he knocked off the bar."

"Oh shit. How much?" Lilah bit her lip. "I don't have any cash."

"Relax, darlin'. Just a shot glass and two pints. Your damage is . . . " Garrett calculated. "Eight bucks."

Lilah stalked over to Danny. "You broke glasses," she said. "Give me a twenty."

The drunk handed Lilah an old leather billfold, clearly so out of it he barely registered the demand. She withdrew a ten and thrust it at Garrett.

"I'm sorry," she murmured. "That was all he had. It's not enough for tip." Her eyes watered and her bottom lip threatened to wobble, but she got them both under control. "Can I take him home now?"

The bouncer propelled Danny towards the door and shoved him outside. "I don't want to see you back here again, Brogan."

"Thank you, Garrett," Lilah said softly, heading after her boyfriend.

"Wait."

She turned back. The sadness on her face was a fist tightly clenching his heart.

"Are you sure you'll be okay?"

Her final words as she slipped out the door didn't reassure him in the least. "I'm always okay."

3 chapter three

DANNY WAS SO mad by the time they got home that he locked her out of the bedroom. “You embarrassed me tonight, Li. I can’t go back there again and I liked that bar.”

“You embarrassed yourself. It’s Valentine’s Day. You ignored me and then got mad when I had a casual conversation with the bartender. You’re an ass and you need to get help. I’m tired of your drinking. I’m tired of a lot of things.” She rested her forehead against the door, the tears burning her eyes. She should leave. Right now. If only she had somewhere to go.

“You don’t get to judge me, bitch. I’m the reason you’ve got a roof over your head. That fancy laptop, your cell phone. You couldn’t afford any of it without me.”

“Please, Danny. Open the door. I’ll make you some coffee. Mac and cheese. We can talk.”

“Fuck you. I’m going to bed. I’m driving myself tomorrow.”

“But your license . . . ” She gave up shouting through the door, trudged into the bathroom, and washed her face. What would it be like to have a boyfriend who didn’t yell? Who didn’t ignore her? Who talked to her like Garrett had talked to her? Who cared that Valentine’s

Day was supposed to be a day for romance, or at least for spending time together.

She dragged herself into the living room, stretched out on the couch with a blanket, and closed her eyes. She could picture him, even now. The dark brown hair, a little shaggy on top but cropped close on the sides. The stubble that lined his jaw, shaved smooth on his cheeks, and the little dent in his square chin when he smiled. Both times she'd seen him, he'd had on a long-sleeved black shirt rolled up to his elbows to reveal his tattoos. The skulls, the lightning bolts, and the roses fascinated her, and she wanted to ask him what they represented. Too bad she'd probably never see him again.

She drifted off to sleep with Garrett's voice in her head. *"Are you sure you'll be okay?"*

No. Not any more.

~

The next day, after her library shift, she took the bus down to Shade's. She'd taken twenty dollars from her emergency stash—the one that she'd started so she could one day leave. It only had a couple hundred dollars in it so far, but it was a start. She wanted to drop off a tip for Garrett—if he was there—since Danny hadn't felt the need to pay a single cent over his bar bill the night before. She didn't know what she was doing, or why—only that she wanted to see Garrett and apologize.

The bar was a different place in the daylight. It was emptier, for one thing. Quieter too. Garrett sat on a stool, nursing a cup of coffee and reading a book. He looked up when she entered and broke into a grin.

"What are you doing here?"

"I came to drop off a tip. You bought me dinner . . ." She dug in her pocket for the twenty and handed it over. "It's not enough. But it's all I have right now."

Garrett stared at the bill, folded it in half, and handed it back to her. "Not necessary, darlin'. We're square. Just tell your boyfriend not to come back in here. You're welcome any time, though."

"This isn't really my—"

Lilah's phone rang in her purse and she fished it out, cringing when she saw Danny's cell number on the screen.

"Excuse me, I have to take this." She answered the phone, her stomach quivering. "Danny?"

Garrett frowned at her, and she turned away, feeling like she'd somehow disappointed him.

"I'm going out with the boys after this next meeting. I'll be home late. Don't wait up."

"But I have my writing group tonight," she said, only barely keeping the whine from her voice. He hated it when she whined. "I need the car."

"Tough. Your writing's shit. No one's going to read it. You're wasting your time with them."

Her fingers tightened around the phone, knuckles white. "Of course. You're right."

The music changed to something more upbeat and Lilah flinched when Danny noticed. "Where are you?" She should have gone outside.

"I'm at the gym," she answered, the lie rolling automatically off her tongue. The gym was her refuge. She claimed she went for two hours every day, but really she stayed at the library and wrote. She never saved anything on her laptop, though. Every file was tucked away on a little USB drive that she kept in the lining of her purse. The silky material had torn three years ago and it made for the perfect hiding place. Danny sometimes went through her emails and her files. The last time he'd found one of her novel drafts, he'd yelled at her for an hour. After that, she'd started tucking money away—a few dollars at a time—and bought the USB drive not long after. Even though her writing wasn't any good, it made her feel better and she wouldn't give it up.

"Good. Stay an extra hour. Those workouts aren't doing shit for you."

The connection dropped and Lilah slid the expensive piece of plastic and glass back in her purse. He provided. She had to remind herself of that. She had clothes—though not stylish ones—a laptop, a new smart phone, heat, food, and shelter. So what if she didn't have love? Or respect? When she turned around, Garrett's arms were crossed and he looked seriously pissed off.

"Sit," he said, the commanding tone somehow managing to sound so much gentler than Danny's ever did. He waited while she arranged herself on the stool and folded her hands on the bar, and then she met his gaze. The space between them disappeared as he leaned in, leaving only inches between her lips and his. His mouth was a firm line. He was a big man. Bigger than Danny. "Not scared of me?"

She eyed the tats covering his forearms and the palms that were bigger than both her hands. "No."

"Then why are you scared of him?"

She jerked, her hip sliding off the stool. Reaching out, instincts on overdrive, she caught Garrett's arm when it shot to steady her. Hard, rippling muscles under her desperate fingers kept her from landing on the floor in a heap.

"Easy, darlin'."

Garrett's slight drawl was roughened by the near catastrophe. His eyes were almost black in the dim overhead lights.

"Thank you."

"You didn't answer my question. Why are you so scared of him?"

"It's complicated."

"Always is. What are you drinkin'? It's on me. Another bourbon?" He turned to browse the bar's collection of bottles.

"Why not? It's not like I have to be anywhere. Danny's out with the guys. He won't be home until late and I want to be asleep when he gets there. It'll make things easier." She lifted a shoulder, unsure why she was admitting all that to Garrett, a man who was certainly dangerous. To her anyway.

Lifting the bottle of Knob Creek and twirling it in his hands, he upended it for a three count into a rocks glass and then slid it towards her. She inhaled its rich, caramel scent, lifted the glass to her lips, and let the spicy bourbon slide down her throat.

"Mmmm. You're spoiling me. Two good drinks in two days. I haven't had a quality bourbon in a couple of years."

"Jesus, Lilah. Get the hell out of there."

The liquid caught in her throat and she fought not to let it come back up. "You don't get to judge me. You don't know me."

"I know an abused woman when I see one," he snapped back.

"Danny has never hit me. Not once. And he's done more for me than you'll ever know." She set the glass down, all desire for a drink gone.

"You're afraid of him. You do what he wants, even when it means you can't do what you want. How long have you been in that writing group of yours?"

"Two years."

"How often do they meet?"

Her voice dropped. "Once a week."

"And how many times have you gone?"

She shook her head.

"How many times, Lilah?" He leaned closer, the scent of leather and something woodsy tickling her nose.

"Five times," she whispered, averting her eyes.

"I rest my case."

"What am I supposed to do, Mr. Know-It-All? Yes, I used to dream about being a writer. But I don't have any talent. Danny needs the car to get to and from work. And I know all of four people in this town. Five if I count you, which I don't, because you're not exactly endearing yourself to me."

"Who told you that you didn't have any talent? Him?"

She blushed, unwilling to answer and confirm his suspicions.

"Dreams don't die, Lilah. Dreams live forever. Unless we let someone else kill them. Don't let anyone kill your dreams."

"*I* killed that dream, Garrett. Not Danny. Me. And it's going to stay dead. I'm a part-time librarian and that's as close to writing books as I'm ever going to get. I don't know what you expect me to do or why the hell you even care." She downed another sip of her bourbon.

"Answer me this. Do you have friends? Close friends?"

"I have Danny."

"That's not an answer. You know how abusers get their victims to stay? They cut them off from their support system. You don't have friends, you don't have dreams. That's abuse. I don't care if he never hits you. He knocked me on my ass last night for standing up to him. How long until he does that to you?" Garrett's knuckles were white, his fingers gripping the bar like a vise.

"I . . ." She didn't have a good response for him. He was right. At least about her friends. She hadn't talked to Irene or Yasmin, her two college roommates, in a year or more. They kept trying to get her to leave Danny and she'd grown tired of defending him and herself. They were right. Garrett was right. She knew it, but that didn't mean she could *do* anything about it. She was trapped. She'd be trapped until she managed to sock away enough for a deposit on an apartment.

"Leave. Now. Hell, I'll drive you to your place, help you pack, and bring you anywhere you want to go. There's got to be a shelter with space."

She laughed. "And what do I tell them? My boyfriend drinks too much and never lays a hand on me? Danny provides a roof over my head, clothes, books, and food and all he ever asks is that I keep myself in shape and cook him dinner? He took care of me after—" Her hand shot up to her mouth and she shook her head. "He's not the greatest guy. I know that. Believe me. I wish he'd tell me I'm good enough the way I am, encourage my writing, buy me flowers, or even tell me I'm not bad looking once in a while, but if those are the only things I want for in life, I've got it pretty damn good."

"There's more to life than getting by. Believe me. I've been there. Barely living. *Existing*. And that's all you're doing, darlin'. Existing."

Lilah reached for the bourbon again, needing the liquor to silence the inner voice Garrett had awoken.

It told her she worth something. That she *should* leave. The voice hadn't shut up since she'd met him. No. This was her life. Danny was all she was ever going to have, unless . . . No. Even if she found another job, she couldn't leave. She didn't have anywhere to go. So what if he drove away any new friend she tried to make? So what if he'd taken away the joy in running, in singing, and in graphic design. She'd been good once. Not at the top of her field, by any means, but well respected. But after she'd designed a logo for his consulting firm—his once popular consulting firm—and he'd berated her in front of his three partners for being unprofessional and a *fucking joke,* she hadn't touched Photoshop again.

"Lilah?"

She'd been off in her own little world. With a quick shake of her head, she brought herself back. "Don't try to save me, Captain America. I don't need it and I certainly don't want it. Thank you for the drink. I did need that. But now I have to go to the grocery store and get home. It was nice—well, no. It wasn't." Sliding off the stool, she slung her bag across her body. "Goodbye, Garrett."

Captain America? It had been a number of years since anyone had called him that. Not since Iraq. After the attack, the army had discharged him and helped him through rehab, and his platoon had checked up on him for a year or two. Now, eight years after his last tour, he really only kept in touch with three of them. Mac, out in Boston, whom he'd met on his very last assignment, Nomar in Portland, and Ed here in Seattle. He glanced at his watch. He was due at the bank for a meeting with Ed and the loan officer in an hour.

"Hey, Matt?" Garrett called out to the junior bartender currently on break in the back. "I gotta get the fuck out of here. Get off your ass."

The young man with the black buzz cut and freckles rushed out. "Sorry 'bout that. I was on the phone with my girl."

"I'll be back by the after-work rush. Don't burn the place down," Garrett said as he grabbed his satchel from behind the bar and slung it over his shoulder.

"One time. One tiny, little fire and you're never going to let me live it down," Matt grumbled.

"Nope. You were lucky it wasn't in the storeroom. Amount of alcohol back there, this place would have lit up like the Fourth of July."

Six months ago, the power had gone out and the kid had used candles rather than the battery-operated table lanterns for light. One of the candles toppled over behind the bar and caught some spilled vodka on the floor. Only Garrett's quick fire extinguisher action had kept the damage localized to one lower cabinet.

With a final grin and a strong urge to ruffle the young man's hair, Garrett ambled out of the bar. He had to see a man about a loan.

Garrett tried to contain his excitement. His dreams were well on their way to coming true. The loan had been approved and he and Ed had an appointment later in the week to take a look at a potential space for their very own bar. As the managing partner, Garrett would own sixty percent of the business. With craft cocktails, gourmet food, and a private event space in the mix, he couldn't wait. Shade's would soon be a distant memory. He whistled along to the Smiths on the radio and turned back onto MLK.

The rain had started in earnest during the meeting and he hunched forward over the steering wheel to see the lines in the road. Driving north towards Shade's, he came around a curve and swore, slamming on his brakes just in time to avoid hitting a trudging figure along the side of the road. When the pedestrian looked up, he swore again. Lilah.

They locked eyes, and he'd never quite seen a woman look so much like a deer in the headlights. Jerking the gearshift into park, he leaned over and unlocked the passenger door. He shoved it open. "Get in!"

She stared at him, shaking her head and backing away.

"Lilah, you're soaked through. Get in. I'll drive you wherever you need to go."

"I'm fine. It's only another mile."

"For fuck's sake. Get in the goddamn truck."

Lilah grabbed the handle on the side of the truck and used it to lever herself up and inside the warm cab. Her bag clutched in the arm she kept drawn across her body looked waterproof, but the rest of her wasn't. A shopping bag was soaked through and half the groceries inside were probably waterlogged.

Garrett reached behind the seat and found a towel for her and then spun the heat up to maximum. Seattle in the winter could be wet, cold, or both, and today was both.

"Thanks," she said, drying her face. She then draped the towel over her head and twisted it around her hair.

"Why the hell were you walking in this weather? I

thought you took the bus." He didn't put the truck in gear, not quite ready to take her anywhere yet.

"The three o'clock bus didn't come. There's only one bus every hour that gets me home, otherwise I have to take three transfers and wait for half an hour in the tunnel. When the bus didn't show, I decided to walk. It's only four miles. Piece of cake when it's dry."

"Where am I taking you?"

"University and Grand."

"Are you sure?"

Lilah frowned. "Yes. I need to go *home*."

"Like hell you do," he muttered, but Garrett put the truck in gear and pulled back onto the road. Lilah curled her body around her bag, shivering. He couldn't turn the heat up any higher and the urge to bring her back to his place, get her dry, and talk some sense into her was almost overwhelming.

"I didn't think it was possible to be this wet," she murmured. "I think my bra is holding water."

The laugh that escaped him probably wasn't what she wanted to hear, but he couldn't help it. She glared through lowered lashes and then stared out the window.

It might have only been a mile, but Seattle's traffic made the drive a full twenty minutes. He savored her scent, wet lilacs, as it filled the cab of the truck, and the way she relaxed as the heat took away the worst of the chill. He'd seen abused women before—up close and personal—and she had all the symptoms. Defensiveness, the careful way she carried herself in public, her rare outbursts of honesty that seemed to surprise her. Not to mention the change in her body language when her phone rang.

A buddy's sister had lost her life to an abusive and violent husband not long after Garrett and Sam's last tour—the one that had taken Garrett's leg and Sam's life. He'd met the girl at Sam's funeral. She'd been a timid little thing. Pretty, but afraid. Garrett had been too wrapped up in his own shit to care that her husband kept a hold of her arm the entire service and berated her more than once for crying. He'd carry that guilt for the rest of his life.

"This is me," Lilah said, pointing to a squat apartment complex with two dozen units. Garrett turned into the parking lot and headed for an open space next to the mailboxes. She unbuckled her seatbelt. "Thanks for the—shit!"

"What?" The panic in her last word wound its way around his heart and he was instantly on alert. He loosened his own seatbelt.

"Danny's home. That's his car. Pull around the back, or a block away or something. Please. Go now."

Garrett was about to put the truck in reverse when Danny Brogan raced out of his apartment on the bottom floor. A look of murderous rage twisted his face. He was at the truck in three steps and had the door open before Garrett could hit the locks. He dragged Lilah out by her arm. The putrid scent of vomit clung to the man.

Garrett flew out of the truck and raced around the front. He wasn't about to leave Lilah to deal with this monster alone. Rain pelted him, soaking into his shirt. He didn't care.

"What the hell are you doing in another man's truck?" Danny shook her and Lilah cringed.

"It was raining, he . . . "

"Take your hands off the lady," Garrett said, his voice gritty and rough. "Before I do it for you."

"You're fucking her, aren't you?"

"What?" The man was delusional. He had to get Lilah away from the asshole, now. She wasn't safe.

"Danny, it's okay. It was only a ride. He didn't touch me," Lilah whimpered, trying to get free. "Please, you're hurting me."

Garrett saw red. That was enough. No one hurt women when he was around. He grabbed Brogan's hand and bent his fingers back to their breaking point, allowing Lilah to tear her arm free. The drunk screamed obscenities at both of them. He'd almost managed to get a hold of Brogan's other hand when a kick to his solar plexus drove the air from his lungs. He stumbled back, tripped over the curb, and went down hard. His head hit the bumper of his truck and stars floated in his vision.

"Danny!" Lilah screamed.

The sound of fists hitting flesh was followed by a pained sob.

"Fucking bitch. Worthless piece of ass."

Another punch and a whimper. Garrett shook his head to clear the cobwebs and pushed to his feet. Lilah cowered against the wall of the apartment building, absorbing blow after blow to her ribs. Blood trickled from her mouth.

"The only worthless one," Garrett said, grunting, "is you, dumbfuck." He spun Danny away, shoving him a good two feet. He wanted to pummel the man into a bloody mess, but that wouldn't help Lilah. Fists raised, he got between them. "Get in the truck, Lilah. Now."

She sank to her knees, retching, crawling towards his truck. Danny went for her, but Garrett was faster. Garret's punch caught Danny hard in the chin, bloodying his mouth much like Danny had bloodied Lilah's. Garrett turned, heading for Lilah, but Danny grabbed him from behind, pinning his arms to his sides. Danny fought with the anger only a desperate man could muster, grabbing Garrett's arms, kicking at his bad leg, catching it in the knee joint, the ankle, and finally the foot. The prosthetic loosened. Not a lot, but enough to throw Garrett off balance again. He stumbled, clutching his thigh where *he* ended and the leg began. In the few seconds it took to ensure he wasn't going to be suddenly legless, Danny released him and then shoved Lilah back into the parking lot. She begged him to stop, but her pleas went unheeded.

The sky took that moment to loose a deluge of frigid, fat drops of water. Lilah threw her arm up to shield her face. Blinded by the rain and a rapidly swelling eye, she ran in the wrong direction, not towards Garrett's truck, but towards the street. Danny gave chase, grabbed the purse still draped across her body, and pulled. Lilah ducked and the purse came free. Her momentum carried her further into the busy street, and Garrett's heart stopped.

She didn't have a chance. Her body flew over the hood of a small sedan. The sickening crunch of bone and flesh hitting metal wrenched a scream from his throat. Lilah landed in a heap a few feet from the car, the rain washing the blood from her pale cheeks.

"You fucking son of a bitch!" Garrett flew at Danny, landing a punch so hard the man fell back, unconscious.

The driver who'd hit Lilah, a young girl of no more than twenty, stumbled out of the car. "Oh my God. Oh my God. I couldn't stop. She came out of nowhere . . . "

"Call 911!" Garrett snapped, dropping awkwardly down next to Lilah. From the way her right leg folded underneath her, he figured she'd broken it in at least two places. "Darlin', open your eyes."

A finger pressed gently against the pulse point at her throat revealed a weak heartbeat. Garrett smoothed a few locks of hair away from her eyes. A gash along the side of her forehead bled profusely. "Lilah, please."

The girl on the phone to 911 sobbed a few feet away while traffic slowed to view the accident. Pounding footsteps from somewhere behind him became a man at Garrett's side. "I'm the apartment manager. What the hell happened? Shit. Lilah."

"Brogan attacked her. Go make sure he doesn't go anywhere. I want him arrested."

The apartment manager marched Danny into the building, muttering about the police and some vaguely obscene things he wanted to do to the cocksucker. The young woman from the car paced and sobbed to her mother on the phone. Time slowed. Garrett prayed. If she died . . . no. He forced that thought away. He wouldn't let that happen. Not if he could stop it.

Lilah whimpered and her eyelids fluttered.

"Come on, darlin'. Come back now. Open those pretty eyes for me."

"Garrett?" The single word was barely audible over the rain and the thundering of his heart, but she focused on him with one eye—the other was nearly swollen shut.

"Don't move, Lilah. Not one inch. The ambulance is on its way."

"Danny. Why?" She tried to raise her head, but the pain must have been too much because she moaned and closed her eyes again.

"Fucking asshat isn't going to hurt you again. I'll kill him myself before I let that happen."

She didn't respond, but the fingers of her left hand flexed and searched for something. When she touched his leg, she fumbled for the denim, a thin whine escaping her swollen lips.

"I'm right here." He took her hand, settling her as the sirens drew closer. The relentless drive of the raindrops carried Lilah's blood down the pavement. There was too much. Her head. Her shoulder. Even her arm. With another whimper, her grip relaxed and her body stilled.

Garrett paced the waiting room of the ER. He'd followed the ambulance to the hospital so he'd have his truck, though he hated to leave Lilah alone. It was probably for the best. The EMTs needed room to work. She wasn't breathing easily and they suspected a collapsed lung.

Now, dressed in a dry pair of scrubs the nurses had dug up for him, he clutched Lilah's phone. He'd retrieved her purse from the parking lot and brought it with him. There were only five saved numbers in her contacts. How could anyone have so few friends? He scrolled through the entries. Pagliacci Pizza, Danny, Library, Irene, and Yasmin. Irene and Yasmin didn't have local numbers, but if they were friends, maybe they'd be able to talk to Lilah—help her stay away from Danny. As much as he wanted to be there for her, liked her, even cared about her, he was a man and what she needed right now was another woman.

"Mr. James?"

He whipped his head around. A short, ruddy man in green scrubs and a polka-dot hat offered him a weary smile. "She's resting. We've set her leg. Two fractures there, both clean breaks, should heal well. She has a hairline fracture to her pelvis, which is going to be pretty damn painful for a few weeks, but she'll be okay. A couple of cracked ribs, one of which collapsed her lung, but we've taken care of that. Her head wound isn't serious. A minor concussion. There'll be a little confusion, maybe disorientation. The bruises and the facial contusions won't look pretty for a while, but they're the least of her worries, I think."

"Can I see her?"

"In a few minutes. The nurse will come get you. We'd normally only let family in, but she asked for you."

Something in his heart warmed and cracked. "Thanks, Doc."

Able to breathe again and hopeful that Lilah wouldn't be too mad at him, Garrett punched the number labeled Irene on Lilah's phone.

A sleepy, husky female voice answered. "Lilah? Is that really you?"

"Hi. You don't know me, but your number was in Lilah's phone."

"Danny Brogan, if you're going through her phone, I am going to call the police right now!" The woman's voice shrilled. Garrett cringed.

"This isn't Danny. He's in jail. My name's Garrett James. Danny beat up Lilah and in the process, pushed her into the path of a car. She's goin' to be okay, but she's in the hospital."

"Oh my God. Shit. *Shit*. I knew it. He's been abusing her all along, hasn't he? Wait. Who the hell are you again?"

"Garrett James. Listen. This is going to need some explanation and I'm waitin' to get in to see Lilah. She broke her leg, fractured her pelvis, and she's got a mild concussion. She's going to need help and I'm not the one to do it. She needs a girlfriend. Someone who can stay with her for a while. Help her. Make sure she presses charges against that fucker. Uh, sorry. Terrible excuse for a human being."

"No, he's a fucker."

They shared a nervous chuckle before Irene continued. "I live in Dayton. Ohio. I lost my job a couple of months ago and money's kind of tight. I'll be there as soon as I can, but last minute flights . . . it might take me a few days to get something I can afford. Those injuries . . . she'll be in the hospital for a bit, right?"

"Probably. What's your last name?"

"Jenkins. Why?"

"As soon as I see Lilah and make sure Danny's not going to be a problem tonight, I'll get you a flight. Are there direct flights from Dayton to Seattle?"

"Yes."

"Whatever the first one is tomorrow, you'll have a seat on it. Lilah's in Harborview Medical Center. You solvent enough to get a hotel or a rental car for a couple of nights if you have to?"

"Who *are* you?" Irene's throaty voice was full of disbelief. "Why the hell would you do that?"

"A few years ago, a buddy's sister lost her life to her abusive husband. Consider this a way to pay off a debt. Lilah doesn't know me. We met a few days ago. Had a couple of good conversations. But I was there when she was attacked. Which is why she's not going to want me around to help pick up the pieces. Once I know she's got someone with her, I can go. She needs to heal, figure out who she is without that asshat and the next couple of days are going to be the hardest for her. Make sure she doesn't go back to him."

"I can get myself a car and a hotel. She'll go back to him over my dead body. If I have to, I'll drag her back to Dayton with me."

"Good." Garrett rattled off his cell phone number for Irene and promised to stay with Lilah until she arrived. When he finished the call, he looked up to see a smiling nurse waiting for his attention.

"You're one of those good guys, aren't you?"

Garrett shrugged. "Doin' what I can. I couldn't stop him from hurtin' her. I can stop her from going back. Or try to anyway."

"She's awake. Pretty out of it, but she should recognize you. Don't be worried about the confusion. It's normal. She's on some powerful pain meds and the head injury doesn't help. She shouldn't talk too long, okay? She's going to be woken up every two hours until the morning, so let her sleep when she can."

"Gotcha."

Garrett followed the nurse down the hall, past a set of security doors, and into the ICU. She gave him an ID bracelet that would let him in and out of the ICU and Lilah's room. He stopped in the doorway. His heart jumped into his throat. The woman in the bed couldn't be Lilah. Her hair disappeared behind the gauze wrapped around her temple. Her face was three shades of purple in spots, pure white in others. A cast surrounded her right leg from a few inches above the knee to her toes. Blankets covered her thin frame, artfully arranged around the cast and the cords and tubes that snaked from her chest and her right arm.

He should have been faster.

The door opened and bright lights spilled into the dim room. Lilah squinted through her one good eye, trying to place the big man heading towards her. He was familiar: the ink on his forearms, the messy dark brown hair, the neatly trimmed stubble. He was safe. He wasn't Danny. He'd helped her earlier.

"Lilah?" His voice was so gentle. Kind. His name was in her head somewhere. What was it?

"What happened to me?" All the doctors had told her was that she'd been hit by a car. They didn't really know why. Or they wouldn't tell her.

"Can I sit down?" He gestured to the chair next to her bed.

She tried to nod, but pain stabbed at her skull. She had four stitches in her scalp. She remembered that. She couldn't raise her head, move her legs, or sit up. Not without pain. Something about her pelvis. The man sat, rested his hand on the bed next to her arm, and stared. She wanted him to touch her, but she didn't know how to ask. She should know his name. George? Grant?

"I gave you a ride home today. It was raining. When we got to your apartment—"

It all came crashing back to her. The fear, the pain. "Danny did this."

"Yeah, darlin'. I'm sorry."

Dreams don't die, darlin'. "You stopped him."

"Not quick enough. Not before he hurt you."

Lilah reached for his hand, wincing at the movement. "Where is he?"

The man tried to pull his hand away and his voice, when he spoke again, was strained. "He's in jail. And I'm going to do whatever I can to make sure he stays there.

The police will probably want to talk to you tomorrow. The doctor told them you weren't up for it tonight."

"He didn't mean it."

"Goddammit, Lilah! You could have died. Stop defending the man." He rose and paced the room. The motion made Lilah dizzy and she turned her head away.

"Stop," she said, tears gathering in her eyes. She couldn't do this now. Everything hurt, but her heart hurt the most. She'd failed somehow. Failed Danny, failed Garrett, and failed herself. *Garrett.* His name was Garrett. "Don't yell." Her plea came out a whimper, desperate and childish.

Garrett cursed quietly. He dropped back into the chair, his hands on his thighs. "I'm sorry. I won't yell again."

"Stay with me," Lilah begged. "I don't want to be alone. But don't ask me to leave him. Not tonight."

Garrett leaned forward and took her hand. His grip was strong and warm. "I'm goin' to ask you tomorrow."

"I'm tired, Garrett."

"Get some sleep, darlin'." He bent over her and pressed a gentle kiss to her forehead. "No one's goin' to hurt you tonight."

Lilah closed her eyes. The hum of the machines and the haze from the drugs comforted her almost as much as his touch. "You won't let him find me here?" she whispered.

"No. I won't."

chapter four

Lilah hated the hospital, but the doctors refused to let her leave until she could get herself to and from the bathroom without assistance. The crutches bruised her armpits, she was dizzy and disoriented half the time from the concussion, and she couldn't even read—doctor's orders. Irene retrieved her laptop and rented a bunch of DVDs to keep her occupied, but she kept falling asleep in the middle of them.

The police came to take her statement the day after the accident—no, the attack—and Danny was in jail. He'd been fired the afternoon he'd hurt her. The firm's partners were done with his drinking and his unprofessional behavior with clients. Losing his job had sent him over the edge, and he'd not only been drunk, but high as well. Cocaine. After a few days of detox, he called her from jail and sobbed over the phone for half an hour, begging her to forgive him.

"He'll change," she told Irene, only to have the television remote snatched from her hand and brandished like a weapon.

"Lilah Jane McKinney, if I ever hear such nonsense coming out of your mouth again, I'm going to break your other leg. That jerkwad put you in the hospital and nearly killed you. You are *not* going back to him. I promised that young man I'd let you do that over my dead body and I meant it."

"Garrett? You talked to him?" Lilah tried to sit up straighter, but her ribs protested and she lay back down, panting.

Irene frowned. "Yes. I did. But we're talking about you now. Not Mr. Cutie. Danny cut you off from your friends, made you feel like shit, and then had the gall to try to kill you."

"I always told myself that I'd leave him if he ever hit me," she said, letting Irene help her sit up so she could eat dinner.

"Well, he did a hell of a lot more than that."

"I know. I'm sorry," she said automatically, though she didn't know what she was apologizing for.

Irene slid the tray of lukewarm meatloaf and Jell-O towards her. "You didn't do anything wrong, sweetie. So don't you go apologizing. That's the jerk talking. Not you. Eat your dinner. We'll talk more about this later."

Two days after the attack, when Irene left to get Lilah some real food—a Dick's cheeseburger and fries—a knock at Lilah's door startled her awake. "Come in?"

"Lilah McKinney? I'm Dr. Denise Lefterts. I'm a therapist at Safe Haven. I'd like to talk to you for a while if you're feeling up to it."

Great. Someone else who's going to ask me to leave Danny. "Fine. Have a seat."

"I'm told that your boyfriend put you in here. Can you tell me what happened?" Dr. Lefterts crossed her long legs and opened a notebook, poising a pen over the paper. She was a thin woman in her fifties, with kindly blue eyes and a heart-shaped face. Her brown hair was cropped short, streaked with gray.

Lilah sighed and recounted the story yet again. Dr. Lefterts asked her questions from time to time—focused, piercing questions that forced Lilah to be honest with herself. Danny didn't love her and she didn't love him.

"What is love?" Dr. Lefterts asked.

"Caring so much for someone that you want their happiness, even if it means you sacrifice your own."

"Did you want Danny to be happy?"

"No. I didn't want him to be mad. He was never happy. Not after I lost the baby. Maybe not even before."

"Did he want you to be happy?"

Lilah closed her eyes, suddenly unwilling to face the doctor. "No. He didn't care what I wanted or needed. God. How could I stay for so long?"

Dr. Lefterts patted her hand. "You're not alone, Lilah. Too many women stay long past the time they should move on. We don't realize how bad things are until it's too late."

"We?" She blinked her eyes open, curious.

"I didn't leave until I started to self-harm. My husband used to grab me hard enough to leave bruises. Not often. Two, three times a year. But one time, he sprained my wrist. The next day I moved wrong and the pain was so intense that I had to sit down. But once it faded, I grabbed my wrist again and twisted. The pain made me feel alive and I hadn't felt that way in a long time. I cut for six months before the blade—before *I* cut too deep and ended up in the hospital. That *mistake* probably saved my life. This attack may have saved yours. If your boyfriend—"

"Ex-boyfriend?" Lilah couldn't keep the wobble from her voice, but it felt good to say the words.

"If your ex-boyfriend"—the doctor smiled—"escalated to drugs, he probably would have hit you again. The rain, the car . . . they saved your life."

"I didn't think he'd go from being a dick to nearly killing me in one afternoon. Piece-of-shit asshat with balls the size of raisins." She couldn't believe she'd said that, but giving voice to *Lilah*, the woman she'd been before Danny, made her feel like herself again, even if she didn't know how long she'd be able to maintain her outrage.

The smell of fast food and a laugh startled them both. Irene grinned from the doorway. "It's good to see you getting some of that Lilah spirit back again, sweetie."

Dr. Lefterts stood. "That's enough for today, Lilah. If you're up for it, I'll come back tomorrow and we can talk more?"

"Okay. That . . . I'd like that."

Dr. Lefterts was as good as her word. Every afternoon at two, she returned, notebook in hand. By the end of the week, Lilah had spoken to the police again and signed the charges against Danny, allowed Irene to pack up her things from the apartment and put them into temporary storage, and applied for aid from Safe Haven. If approved, she'd get two thousand dollars to use to start over—a deposit on a new apartment and help for her medical bills. Danny wasn't getting out of jail any time soon, but his was the only name on the lease. The landlord offered to change the locks and let her stay, but that place held too many memories. "It's over. I can't go back.

I need a new place. And it's got to be cheap. My library job won't pay the bills."

Safe Haven had a list of apartment complexes that provided subsidized rent to battered women, and though Lilah hated to admit it, that's what she was. She and Irene looked at photos on Safe Haven's website and picked the complex with the best rating. Lilah signed a three-month lease the day Danny was arraigned and moved into her new home two days later, the day she was released from the hospital. Irene oversaw the delivery of a new bed, courtesy of Yasmin, a successful corporate lawyer in San Francisco. Irene and Lilah lay side by side that night, Lilah's broken leg supported by pillows, in an otherwise empty apartment that was hers and hers alone.

Irene patted her hand. "I've missed you, Lilah."

"*I've* missed me. But I don't feel like I'm really here. I don't know who I am any more. Not without him."

"You're Lilah McKinney. You're a writer, a kick-ass designer. You're funny as hell when you want to be. You loved to run, to read, and to cook. You're gorgeous and kind, and you can sing like an angel."

"That's not the person Jerkface wanted." She didn't want to use his name, and had taken to calling him Jerkface to Irene and to herself. She'd slipped up once and said the word to Dr. Lefterts, earning a laugh and a "Brava!" in response.

"Jerkface doesn't get a say any more. Only you do. Well, and me, but the only thing I'm going to insist on is that you keep seeing the therapist and testify at Danny's trial."

"I will. I promise."

"When the doctor lets you work again, will you go back to your writing? I know Jerkface kept telling you that you were shit, but I think you're really talented. You always dreamed about publishing."

Lightning flashed over a copse of evergreens outside her window, reminding her of Garrett's tattoos. "Dreams don't die," Lilah said.

"What?"

"Something Garrett said. I wish I'd met him some other time. A couple of years ago, maybe. Before I got pregnant. Before I lost the baby. I think we could have been friends."

"I don't think you should see him, Lilah. Not now. You're too vulnerable and he's . . . he's too damn cute and *nice* for you to be objective. You need to learn how to be on your own. How to be Lilah."

"I know." The counselor had told her the same thing. Garrett had disappeared within twenty minutes of Irene's arrival with a kiss to her forehead and a vague "Take care of yourself, darlin'" to remember him by. She'd give it a year—give *herself* a year—to work on Lilah before she'd even consider dating anyone. But she couldn't get that quote out of her head. *Dreams don't die.*

The trial was quick. Lilah made her way to the stand on crutches, sat awkwardly, and told her side of the story. Danny glared at her the entire time. Apparently once she stopped taking his calls, he abandoned all pretenses of being nice. Her voice shook more than once, particularly when Danny's lawyer cross-examined her, but her story never wavered.

On her way out of the courtroom, she thought she caught a glimpse of Garrett, but she couldn't be certain. Even though she ached to talk to him again, to see that easy smile, the brown eyes that crinkled around the edges, the strong, tattooed arms, she dismissed the idea. *Work on Lilah. Find yourself before you do anything else.*

She'd given up seeing him, but his words were always with her. A month after the attack, she walked into Artful Dodger Tattoo & Comics and walked out with the words *Dreams don't die* on the inside of her right wrist. She'd never let anyone kill her dreams again.

chapter five

Eleven Months Later

Libations. Garrett stared up at the neon sign outside the bar. *His* bar. After six years of working his ass off, he'd managed to achieve his dream. He and Ed had planned to open six months ago, but a sinkhole close to the new tunnel had condemned their chosen space and they'd had to start their search all over again. Ed had pulled out—unable to weather the delay financially. But Garrett had socked away every penny of his tips for five years at Shade's. He'd quit that dump before the original location had fallen through, and picked up shifts at a dozen other bars as a floating fill-in until he found the perfect spot for Libations. Then he worked non-stop for months to get the place ready. It had been almost as stressful as being deep inside Iraq, with less sand and shooting. Cooler too, even when he spent twenty-four hours straight in the middle of a heat wave clearing out the old dry wall, glass, and plywood from the restaurant that'd been in this spot before. Though in Iraq, he hadn't had to deal with the rain and thus, the leaky roof the day after Christmas.

January was a terrible time to open a bar, but that's when all of the permits had come through and making some money was better than none. He hoped everyone who'd given up drinking for the month (who knew that was a Seattle tradition?) would come in for his craft shrubs and the menu his chef Luna had designed to go with Garrett's selection of cocktails.

The grand opening had been a week ago, and today was the first day he'd managed to tear himself away for a much-needed visit to the prosthetic clinic. His leg had given him trouble for months—eleven months to be exact—ever since that fuckwit boyfriend of Lilah's had kicked him after using her as a punching bag.

Lilah. Lilah McKinney. Why did he still remember her name? He hadn't seen her since last February, the day he'd left her hospital room. The pure despair on her face had killed him. She hadn't wanted him to leave, but he wasn't what she'd needed then. In fact, he was the opposite of what she'd needed.

"Stop it," he growled to himself. He'd tried to call her once to check on her, but her number had been disconnected. Probably for the best. At least that asshat was in jail the last he'd checked. He hoped she'd moved on and was happy. She had something, a spark that he knew would shine when she got away from *him*.

Garrett shook his head to rid himself of the memory and pulled open the door of Libations. Business was good for a Tuesday evening. Six patrons sat at the bar with colorful drinks in front of them, chatting. Another dozen people filled the tables, plates of house-cured meats, sliders, popcorn, and roasted Brussels sprouts among them. His assistant bartender Ro—a tattooed, pierced, and dyed Seattleite to her core—spun bottles and winked at one of the more handsome men at the end of the bar. She was a great hire. She'd learned every one of his signature drinks in a single night, and had come up with one or two of her own to fill out the menu. The customers seemed to like her as well, though her appearance did occasionally give one or two of the more conservative businessmen and women pause. But five minutes after sitting down, she'd have them at ease and laughing.

"Hey, Ro," he said, tucking his coat in a cabinet under the bar and taking his customary spot to her right. "Backed up at all?"

"Yeah, I've got three tickets waiting," she replied, nodding towards the computer. "All your libs."

Garrett cringed. Ro's one annoying trait was that she shortened the name of the bar, and his drinks, to Libs. Apparently libations was a waste of two syllables. He punched the screen and brought up the tickets. He took the first one and smiled.

Table Eight: Three SLWK

His signature drink, the one he was the proudest of, was called Seattle's Long Wet Kiss. He'd only come up with the recipe a few months ago, after a mostly sleepless night punctuated by dreams of Lilah. He grabbed bottles, twirled them in a practiced, smooth motion, and filled the cocktail shakers with bourbon, peach liquor, and ginger simple syrup. Shaking each in turn, he drained them into rocks glasses, garnished them with an orange peel twist, and arranged them on a tray. Scanning the bar for one of his servers, he found both were engaged with customers. His leg was tuned, which made walking a hell of a lot easier. He'd deliver the drinks himself.

Table eight was a trio of women in business dress. Two brunettes and a strawberry blond. A plate of bacon-wrapped, stuffed dates lay between them. The blond had her back to him, but from the shake of her shoulders and the reactions of the other two, she was laughing. Her companions were lovely: one a classic raven-haired beauty with wide eyes and high cheekbones. The other was a dark-skinned, lush goddess who was probably six feet tall. He chided himself for gawking, but he was a red-blooded male and he hadn't so much as taken a woman on a second date in more than two years. Either they ran at the idea of dating an amputee or they simply couldn't carry on an intelligent conversation. *Except for Debra.* Debra had been interesting and didn't seem to have a problem with his stump. But she did have a problem with him working every night at a bar. That had lasted two weeks, though they'd only had a single date due to his schedule. At least that dinner date had ended with breakfast the next morning.

"Ladies, three Seattle's Long Wet—"

"Garrett?"

Lilah McKinney's chair wobbled from the speed of her ascent, and she took two quick steps back. She was still as beautiful as she'd been a year ago. No. More. There was a pink scar along the side of her temple from the attack, but otherwise, there appeared to be no ill effects. Not from how quickly she'd moved. Her moss green eyes widened, fear emerging in their depths.

"What are you doing here?" *Duh, idiot. She's having a drink. Try to come up with something more interesting to say. Now.* "Uh, I mean, how are you?" *Not much better. Think!*

"Lilah, you *know* him?" The exotic beauty batted her eyelashes at Garrett. "Introduce us."

A blush flamed on Lilah's cheeks and traveled down her neck to her chest. She wore a sweater the color of her eyes that scooped gently around a pair of breasts he bet would fit into his hands quite nicely. Her black pants showcased a firm, smaller-than-the-last-time-he'd-seen-it ass and she wore a pair of black heels that put her close to his eye level.

"I'm Garrett James," he said, when Lilah didn't make a sound. Flashing his smile, he watched Lilah for a reaction. "I own Libations."

"You what?" Lilah grabbed the back of her chair. The blush faded and she was now paler than he liked—almost as pale as she'd been that last day he'd seen her. She swayed a little, her pupils dilating. Garrett set the tray down on the table and took her arm. She flinched, but leaned into him, her body giving off such mixed signals that he couldn't tell whether she wanted to slap him, run from him, or kiss him.

"Lilah?" The raven-haired woman slid her chair back, but Garrett held up his hand.

"Darlin', come into the back office and sit down for a few. I'll get you some water. It's quiet and we can talk. Ladies, I'll have her back to you in ten minutes. Drinks are on the house."

He didn't give anyone time to protest as he steered Lilah through the bar and into his private office. She didn't resist, resting her head on his shoulder, shaking like a leaf.

"Sit." He didn't want to let her go, but he had to. Helping her into a chair, his hand lingered on her arm, his gaze taking in every inch of her face. The shallow breathing, the trembling lips. From a small fridge, he withdrew a bottle of water, cracked the seal, and then pressed it into her hands. "Drink. It'll help."

She complied, and the color slowly returned to her

cheeks. "Sorry," she murmured. "I'm not usually the swooning type."

"Swooning? Over me?" He swallowed hard, leaning against his desk and clutching its edge to stop himself from reaching out to touch her again. Swooning was good, wasn't it? He'd spent the past year dreaming of her. Had she been dreaming of him?

With pursed lips, she capped the water and set it down next to his hip a little harder than necessary. "For your information, *stud*, swooning means fainting. You surprised me, that's all. And I don't deal with surprises well."

He recoiled. "Lilah, I . . . " He didn't know what to say. He had questions. What was she doing in his bar? What happened after he left her in the hospital? "I tried to call you. After. I worried, but I didn't want to pry. Or dredge up bad memories. Even went by your apartment once, but no one answered."

She reached for the water again, stared at it, and put it down. "Can I have something stronger?"

"Darlin', you can have anything you want. But I don't want to keep you from your girlfriends. I wouldn't be surprised if they break down my door in a few minutes. If you want to stay and talk, if you trust me, go tell them you're okay and I'll pour you the best scotch in the house." He didn't want her to disappear again, but he'd be damned if he was going to get her to stay by intimidation or even guilt.

"Okay." The meek tone didn't sit well with him. This wasn't the Lilah he'd hoped to find. The one who'd called him *stud* was the Lilah he wanted.

Garrett dropped down to one knee and took her hand. She flinched and he wanted to kick himself, but he wouldn't let go of her hand if his life depended on it. "I mean it, Lilah. If you don't want to stay, go back to your friends. I'll even hide out in here until Ro tells me you've gone."

"I changed my cell number," she said, the words tumbling out in a rush. "So he couldn't call me from jail. I never returned to the apartment. Not once. Irene packed my stuff for me. The shelter"—she shuddered and cleared her throat—"helped me get into a new place. I went back to Shade's after I got off the crutches, but you were gone and they didn't know where I could find you. I wanted to thank you." She pulled her hand away, clearly uncomfortable, and flicked a nervous gaze to the door.

"I left to start this place. Took me a while." He stood and jerked the door open. "Go, Lilah. If you want to talk to me, any time, you know where I am now. I'm here every night but Mondays. I'll pour you a drink and listen to anything you have to say. But not when you're looking at that door like it's your lord and savior. I don't ever want you scared of me."

"I . . . I'm sorry," she whispered, bolting for the hall and her friends.

Good job, man. You trapped an abused woman in your office. Way to fuck up. Garrett wasn't sure if he should go back out to the bar, but a quick glance told him Ro was slammed, and leaving her there alone wasn't the responsible thing to do. With a quick word to one of his servers to retrieve the tray he'd left at Lilah's table, Garrett took his place back behind the bar and got to work.

~

Lilah's hands shook in her lap. Her friends sat quietly, waiting for her to explain.

"He saved my life," she said, after taking a generous sip of her Long Wet Kiss. The drink description, coupled with the knowledge that Garrett owned this place, had been the cause of her near-fainting spell. *Made in honor of the only woman the owner wishes he'd had the chance to kiss. Her drink was bourbon, and her voice was honey. Knob Creek, peach liquor, lemon-sage bitters, splash of grenadine. On the rocks.*

"How? And how come you didn't know he owned this place?" Jennifer leaned forward on the table, her dark gaze flitting between Garrett at the bar and Lilah.

"He's the one who called the cops on Danny after the attack. Knocked him out cold."

"Oh! The hottie you said you could never find again." Maura took a sip of her drink, glanced down at the menu, and nearly spit out the amber liquid. "Oh my God, Lilah. Is this drink about *you?*"

"I don't know. I wasn't in any sort of head space to figure out if he liked me back then. I was with Danny. I didn't think I was *worth* anything. Why would anyone like me? And even if I had known, I was *with* Danny. He hated the idea of me even talking to another man, let alone getting to know one."

"But you're not with the jerk now. And Hottie keeps staring over here between mixing drinks. What happened when he took you back to his office? Please tell me you kissed him."

"No. I sort of freaked out on him a little." Lilah filled her girlfriends in on the conversation, short as it was. "I need to ask you a favor."

"Anything as long as it involves you being safe," Maura replied.

"I owe him an explanation. And more than that, I want to give him one. He helped me, and he's the reason I had the support I needed to get out of there. He paid to fly Irene out to Seattle. If he can spare the time, I'll take it. Don't wait for me. I'll call a cab to get home if it's late and I'll text you both when I leave so you know I'm okay."

Her friends worried about her after the string of bad dates she'd had over the past month. She'd started dating again only a few weeks ago, with her therapist's blessing, and had gone on two blind dates and a dinner with a coworker from a different department. Her last fix-up had been an ass—ordering her food, ignoring her protests that she hated zucchini, and belittling her work. She'd thrown a glass of water in his face before the entrees arrived and had stormed out, maintaining her indignation until she'd climbed into bed that night. She'd cried herself to sleep, and memories of Danny haunted her dreams. Talking to men was difficult for her. Hell, talking to anyone was a challenge some days, but she forced herself. She'd come a long way this year, and she *did* trust Garrett. He wouldn't hurt her.

"Earth to Lilah," Maura called, waving her hand. "I said, 'We're not leaving yet. We'll have another round of drinks and more food first.' You tell Hottie—"

"Garrett," Lilah interjected. "Please don't call him Hottie."

"Fine. Tell *Garrett* that if he hurts you, we're going to kick his ass into next week, no matter how hot he is."

Lilah reached out to squeeze their hands. "I know we haven't been close for long," she said, "but I really love you guys."

"We want you to be happy, Lilah. That's all we care about. Be careful and see if he's the guy you remember. And if so, live a little. Maybe kiss him." Jennifer patted her hand. "Go get the guy."

"I'm going to start by talking to him without fainting. If that goes well, I'll see."

Lilah shoved her hands in her pockets, clenching them into fists so she could dig her nails into her palms on the way to the bar. She needed the slight pain to distract her and keep her upright. Garrett's dark brown eyes locked on hers. She could do this. She could talk to the man she'd dreamed about more than once in the past year. He looked the same. A little thinner, maybe. Rough around the edges. A few tiny lines at the corner of his eyes hadn't been there before. He was every bit as handsome as she'd made him out to be in her dreams.

Garrett broke eye contact when Lilah slid a hip onto a barstool. He spun around, grabbed a bottle of Macallan 18 and two glasses, and signaled to the tattooed, pierced woman at the other end of the bar. "I'll be upstairs on break."

Lilah followed him to the back corner of the space, where a metal staircase spiraled up to the second floor. A velvet rope with a sign proclaimed it *The Highball Room, Reserved for Private Parties.* Garrett dropped the rope and took the stairs stiffly, his left leg working a little slower than his right. She wondered what had happened in Iraq, how he dealt with it, and if it pained him or bothered him. Memories of Danny kicking Garrett's leg out from under him swam in her mind until they reached the top of the stairs.

A warm, inviting loft spread out before them. Intimate sets of comfortable chairs and tables filled the space.

Dark wood floors, soft lighting, and antique table lamps beckoned. He flicked a switch on the wall. In the far corner, a gas fireplace crackled to life, bathing the room in an orange glow.

Picking one of the tables close to the fire, Garrett plopped down the glasses and twisted the stopper out of the bottle. He poured them each a generous shot and dropped into one of the chairs, watching her.

"Danny got three years," Lilah said quietly as she picked up the glass and took a timid sip. The caramel-colored liquid went down easily. Too easily. Would her story be as easy to swallow? "Irene reached out to Safe Haven, the battered women's shelter up in Shoreline." She took another sip and tried to smile. "She stayed with me for two weeks. Dealt with the lawyer, got me a therapist, tossed all of Danny's belongings in the trash and packed my things—all while I was in the hospital. She called another friend of ours, Yasmin, in San Francisco, and got her to come up and stay with me for another month. By the time Yasmin left, I was down to a walking boot. I had a job, a new apartment, courtesy of Safe Haven, and a little bit of my life back."

"What do you do?"

She smiled. The expression felt foreign, even though she smiled regularly now. She didn't think she'd ever get used to being happy. "I'm a graphic designer for Stanby and Associates. I do restaurants, coffee shops, and bookstores, primarily. One of Danny's bosses—the one who fired his ass that last day—got me the interview. He might have gotten me the job too, but even if he did, *I've* kept it." Her shoulders straightened. She was good at her job—great even. Not bad for a woman who didn't think she had a single marketable skill a year ago.

Garrett whistled. Stanby and Associates was the premiere design firm in the city. "That's great, Lilah."

Silence filled the room, despite the low buzz of conversation and clinking glasses from downstairs. The scotch warmed her belly, but it didn't make her words any easier. "I shouldn't have stayed as long as I did. I didn't think I was worth . . . anything. Danny broke me down, over four years, so I wouldn't leave him. I didn't know it at the time, but he's a drug addict in addition to an alcoholic. He got fired that last day and switched from pot to cocaine. I think that's why he got violent."

After a vicious sip of his scotch, Garrett glared at her. "Don't make excuses for him."

"I'm not. It's an explanation. Not an excuse. They're different things." She bristled and ran a hand through her hair. She'd cut it after she'd gotten out of the hospital and it fell to her shoulders now. "I know what he did to me, Garrett. I testified against him at his trial. I'm not the same person you met at Shade's. Hell, I wasn't a person back then. Not really. I was Danny's girlfriend. Now, I'm Lilah." She held out her hand.

Garrett shook it, his big hand dwarfing hers. His fingers were rough and strong, and she hung on a second or two longer than necessary, turning her hand slightly so his rested on top of hers.

"It's good to meet you, Lilah."

She liked the way he said her name. Slow and careful, almost like a prayer. He looked down at their hands. The ink on the inside of her wrist peeked from her sweater.

"You didn't have this before," he said, twisting her hand gently and raising a brow as he touched her wrist.

A light tug of her sweater revealed the script. *Dreams don't die.*

"I like it."

There was something to his tone she couldn't place. Shock, maybe? "You said that to me. The day . . . " She shook her head. "I wanted the reminder. I won't let someone take my dreams away again. They're mine and they're important. Even if they never come true, I have to try."

"What do you dream of?" His voice was rough and he took another swig of scotch, watching her with an intense stare. He hadn't let go of her hand and she didn't want him to.

"A lot of things. Going to Rome. Ireland. Buying a house. Love." She looked down, the smile tugging at her lips. "Publishing another book."

"Another?"

"I released my first one a few months ago. It's doing well. I submitted it to a couple of contests and it won an award for best debut novel."

"That's great, darlin'. I'm proud of you."

Those seven little words meant more to her than any of the rare compliments she'd received from Danny. Maybe because Garrett wasn't lying. His warm brown eyes held nothing but honesty.

"Garrett!" A female voice called up the stairs and he pulled his hand away. "Luna's asking for you. She needs to eighty-six the dates."

"That's my chef." He stood, shoving his hands in his pockets, peering over the balcony. "Your friends look like they're paying their bill. Do you have to go?"

"No."

The look of relief on his face melted her heart. "I'll be right back."

When she was alone, she waved to her friends and

then texted Maura. *Staying to talk to Garrett. Don't wait for me.*

Good for you. Text me when you get home.

What would Dr. Lefterts say? Would she approve? True, Garrett was from her life before the attack and Lilah had made it a point not to keep much of that life. Her writing, a few books, a CD or two. She kept in touch with two of Danny's former bosses—the one who'd arranged for her interview and another who'd paid her handsomely for the logo concepts she'd done for them years ago. They'd wanted to keep working with her to cement one of the ideas, though they couldn't decide which one. Danny had taken their indecision as evidence that Lilah had no talent and berated her for it for a month until she quit. He'd taken away the one thing she'd known she was good at. She understood now that Danny was a serial abuser. He needed her weak so he could feel in control.

Now, *she* was in control. She did what she wanted with her life. And right now, she wanted to get to know Garrett.

The gas fireplace warmed and calmed her. She'd always wanted a fireplace. Her apartment didn't have one. At least her place had a view of Lake Washington. But it was winter now, only a month or so before the anniversary of leaving *him*. The bar was already decorated for Valentine's Day. Red candles on all of the tables, red lights dotting the windows in elegant frames. She wondered if she'd ever celebrate Valentine's Day again. She'd loved the holiday before Danny. She couldn't see loving it again. Her wandering thoughts soured her stomach. No. This was time for her to live in the present, not dwell in the past. Curling her legs closer, she swirled the last of the scotch in her glass. "My dreams matter. I matter."

"Of course you matter." Garrett stood at the top of the stairs, a stern look on his face. "Did I make you feel otherwise?"

"No!" Lilah gestured to the chair across from her and waited for Garrett to sit. "It's my mantra. A meditation of sorts, I guess. When I get nervous, when things get bad, it calms me down."

"I don't want to make you nervous."

"Everything makes me nervous, Garrett. Walking out my door in the morning, speaking up in a meeting . . . everything. And the bar—it's all decorated for Valentine's Day. Not my favorite holiday. Bad memories pop up from time to time. But I'm working on it. Every day I get better."

"We could go somewhere else?"

"No. I want to be here. This is yours. And it's beautiful. Tell me how you went from working at a dive bar to owning this." Lilah waved her hand at the space. "There's a lot I don't know about you. Like . . . almost everything."

Two hours later, Garrett had told her all about opening Libations. Lilah had been content to let him talk about himself, but he wanted to get to know her as well. "Tell me about the book."

"I started writing it a few years ago. Kind of like therapy. I couldn't leave him, but I could escape into my writing. I had to hide it. He made fun of me for even *thinking* I could publish one day."

Garrett clenched his fists on the arms of the chair. Leaning forward, Lilah brushed her fingers against his until he relaxed.

"Once I was in my own place and Danny had been sentenced, I started to feel safe. I didn't have to escape any more. But re-reading what I'd written helped me see how poorly he'd treated me. It helped me stay strong. I found an editor, sent her the book, and waited. I wanted to give up when I got her notes back. I thought all her changes meant I wasn't any good. I called my therapist sobbing, convinced Danny had been right about me all along. It took a couple of weeks for me to work up the courage to go back and revise it. But I'm glad I did. I finished the second book last week. That's why we were all out tonight. Celebrating."

The bar buzz started to die downstairs. "I should get home," she said, stifling a yawn. "I have to be at work at eight."

"Are you okay driving?" Garrett asked.

"I don't own a car. I'll take a bus. I'm used to it."

"It's cold. I could . . . take you home. If you're okay waiting a few minutes for me to make sure Ro can close up?"

"I . . . "

"You have someone waiting for you at home. Dammit. I'm sorry. I'll call you a cab. My treat. I don't like the idea of you taking a bus this late." Garrett picked up the bottle of scotch and stalked down the stairs, his shoulders hunched around his ears.

"Garrett, wait." Lilah ran after him, hoping she wouldn't trip in her heels. But he was quick, despite his slightly jerky gait. She didn't catch up to him until she reached the bottom of the stairs. She took his arm. "Don't run away from me."

"I can't do this again," he growled.

"What?"

"Start to care about you when you're with someone else."

She gasped, stepping back and dropping his arm. He

went back to the bar and picked up a cordless phone, leaving her with her mouth hanging open. He cared. *Of course he does. He paid to fly Irene out for you. Stayed with you all night in the hospital.*

"I'm not with anyone," she called out over the din of the few patrons left in the bar.

Garrett whirled around, phone still held to his ear. She got to the bar in time to hear him say, "Hang on." With the phone tucked to his chest, he leaned forward.

"I live close to Kenmore, a few blocks from Third Place Books."

"Never mind. We don't need a cab." He set the phone down. "Wait here, okay?"

Her nod sent him off to the far end of the bar, where he talked quietly to Ro. She glanced over at Lilah a couple of times, grinned, and patted Garrett on the arm. She shoved him towards Lilah with a final slap on the ass. He glared, but didn't hold it. By the time he reached her and retrieved his keys and his leather jacket, he was practically beaming.

"Let's go."

Garrett rested his hand lightly on the small of her back, guiding her out the door and to his truck. Lilah couldn't help but remember the last time she'd been in this truck. The day everything changed. The worst day of her life. "I never asked, but I wanted to. Before. This truck is custom?"

Garrett snapped his seatbelt into place and revved the engine, turning the heat up. "Yeah. I can legally drive with my right leg, but it's technical. With my left, I can feel the road. Drivin' is one of the hardest things to learn to do with a prosthetic. You don't realize how much of it is based on how the pedals feel under your feet. I love drivin'. I wasn't going to let anyone take that away from me."

"What happened?"

Garrett pulled onto Lake City Way and glanced over at Lilah. The flash of street lights illuminated his dark eyes—his quick and intense stare. "It's not a good story, Lilah."

"Does that mean you don't want to tell it or you don't want me to hear it?"

He shrugged, hunched over the steering wheel a little further, and cracked his neck. "Rocket-propelled grenade. Five of us were in a Humvee, routine patrol. The bomb ripped apart the base of the vehicle. I was thrown a dozen feet away. A second grenade hit and half of the engine landed on my right leg. Crushed it. Only thing that stopped me from dyin' was a buddy of mine putting a tourniquet on mid-thigh. But what saved my life also took my leg. No blood flow for too long. Leg ends about here." Garrett rapped on his thigh, halfway between his hip and his knee. The solid sound of the prosthetic echoed in the cab.

"When?"

"Eight years ago."

"What did you do in the army?"

"Just your run-of-the-mill soldier, darlin'. Never rose above specialist. Wanted to, but I was injured only two years into service. Saw enough combat for one lifetime, though."

Silence descended as thick as the fog outside the truck. January in Seattle was typically frigid, but they'd had a short warming spell this week and that brought the fog. The truck's headlights reflected against the white, illuminating Garrett's face. He slowed, approaching 175th.

"Turn right here and then it's the third left. Lake View Apartments."

"Got it."

Garrett parked next to the apartment's exterior stairs. "Lilah," he said, his voice thick and raspy. He cleared his throat, staring over the steering wheel, his hands clenched on his thighs. "Walkin' away from you that day in the hospital was the hardest thing I've ever done. Harder than learnin' to walk with my new leg. I didn't think I'd ever see you again. But then you're in my bar and suddenly nothing else matters but you—talkin' to you, drivin' you home, gettin' your number so I can talk to you again. I want the chance to get to know you and I sure as shit don't want to say good night and never see you again. But you have to tell me what *you* want. If you tell me to leave you alone, I will. I'll walk away."

Lilah reached over and touched his arm. She traced one of the lightning bolts above his wrist. "Give me your phone."

He handed it over without question and let her fiddle with the screen. When she handed it back, it was open to her contact details. Name, phone number, and email address.

"I have to take things slow, Garrett. I have triggers. I have bad days. But . . . " A hot flush reddened her cheeks, sending goose bumps down her arms and up her neck as she tugged at her sweater. "I want to see you again."

He grinned, the motion crinkling his eyes and darkening the dimple in his chin. "Then you'll see me again. Can I walk you to your door? Is that too fast? Too much?"

The laughter bubbled up, unbidden. "No. I think I can handle that without bolting."

He jumped out of the truck and loped around to her

door. He opened it and offered to help her down. "I have Saturday afternoons and Monday nights off," he said when they climbed her stairs and stood in front of her door. "What do you like to do for fun?"

"I'm still figuring that out. But I like the driving range. It's heated. Smacking a little white ball around is a good stress reliever for me. Balls and burgers?"

An odd expression crossed his face, almost a frown, his brows knitting for a brief moment. "I . . . uh . . . I don't know that I can swing a club too well. The torque on my leg might be difficult. You have to promise not to laugh if I suck."

Panic fluttered in her belly as she tried to come up with another idea. "We can do something else," she said quickly, taking a step back.

"No." The single word came out as a growl and Lilah stifled a gasp. He softened his voice, holding up his hands. "Lilah, I want to spend the afternoon with you, doing whatever you want to do."

"But . . . "

"No buts. I've never tried golf. Maybe it'll be fine. And if it's not, we'll do something else next time. You're in charge."

"You're sure?" The look on his face as he nodded reassured her. "Okay. I'll be ready at three. Will you pick me up or should I meet you there?"

"I'll be here at three."

Garrett leaned against the wall, watching her unlock her door. The heat from her small apartment washed over them and she shivered. She was about to step inside when she met Garrett's eyes. She'd never seen them this dark. He scanned her living room, taking in the simple gray sofa, the coffee table with her laptop, and the tiny kitchen.

"Good night, Lilah."

She dropped her purse inside the door, but she couldn't go inside yet. She'd wondered for a year what it would have been like to kiss him and now he was standing in front of her, looking like he was about to implode. He wasn't making a move. Was he going to? Was she? Could she? What if he rejected her? She didn't think she could stand that. It was better if she didn't risk it. "Good night, Garrett."

After slipping inside, she shut the door quickly, her heart beating erratically against her chest. She pressed her cheek against the door to look through the peephole. He hadn't left. His hand touched her door for a moment before he let it fall and turned to walk away.

"I want this," she said to herself and threw open the door. "Garrett."

He turned on a heel and covered the three steps back to her in a single breath. Garrett slid his arm around her back, pulling her close. His rough palm cupped her cheek with a gentleness she didn't expect. She acquiesced to his demanding lips, the trimmed mustache tickling her skin. The scent of him surrounded her: bourbon and leather. Desire quivered in her chest, driving her to take control, something she'd never done before. She slid her fingers through his hair, holding him in place while she explored with her lips and her tongue. Breathless, she only pulled away when the bulge in his jeans couldn't be ignored.

"I wish I could give you more tonight, Garrett. But I can't. I want to do this right. For me. If I move too fast, I'll screw this up—screw myself up."

He brushed a few errant locks away from her eyes. The tender gesture melted her heart. With a chaste kiss to her cheek, he said, "Don't apologize. Don't *ever* apologize for what you need, darlin'. One of my dreams came true tonight. If you want to feel sorry for somethin', feel sorry for all the menus I'm going to have to redo to change the story behind the Long Wet Kiss."

With a laugh, she lightly brushed her lips to his again, and slipped into her apartment. Her entire body tingled from the memory of the kiss. She touched her lips, licked them, tasting him. She watched his grinning form walk down the stairs.

The chime of her cell phone startled her and she fumbled in her purse.

You gave me your number, but I wanted you to have mine. Sleep well, Lilah. Dream of good things.

Oh, she would. And maybe she'd dream of him. Who was she kidding? Of course she'd dream of him.

chapter six

LILAH WOKE UP with a smile on her face. She had a *date*. With Garrett James. She couldn't count the number of times she'd thought of him over the past year. His good-bye to her in the hospital had been terse and full of worry—for both of them. She hadn't yet decided to leave Danny and Garrett had been angry. Or worried. Or some combination of both.

She'd always lamented that she hadn't been able to let him know that Danny was long gone. Had he been at the trial? She'd have to remember to ask.

Two a.m. had come with a dream that left her moaning and highly aroused. It started with Garrett's kiss and ended with her naked. His body was largely a blur. What did he look like without his shirt? Or his pants? The hard muscles of his chest and strong arms holding her tight were all she had to go on. That and some cursory research online about prosthetic legs. How much of him was tattooed? And would she find out?

A scan of her apartment on her way out the door left her feeling insecure. It was a tiny place, though it was all hers. The sofa, the dresser, the coffee table, and the lamps were from Goodwill and though they were in good condition, they were obviously used and mismatched. She had a few pictures: her parents on vacation in San Diego a few years before their deaths, a print of the Seattle skyline, and the cover of her first book. The kitchen was barely large enough for two people, but it worked well enough for her. Only her bed was new and luxurious. Yasmin had bought her one of the best mattresses on the market, and though Lilah had protested the expense, she did love it. The television was Yasmin's doing as well. Her former college roommate, now a successful corporate lawyer, had taken a month off from work to stay with Lilah while she recovered and had refused to be without her soap operas.

Now, almost a year after leaving Danny, her job paid her enough to live on, and even allowed her to save a bit. She used her royalties for entertainment money, but she didn't consider herself flush with cash. After being dependent on Danny for everything, the idea of spending money on frivolous things like new furniture and artwork didn't sit well. Her one splurge was the eight-hundred-thread-count sheets. If she did let Garrett into her space, at least they'd be comfortable in bed. If he didn't run first.

She didn't need much and had never been self-conscious about her place before. But her friends knew her history and she rarely invited anyone over. Her space was her own. Sacred. Her little sanctuary, even if it was plain. After living with Danny for years and being surrounded by *his* things, she'd had a hard time figuring out what *she* liked. So far, she knew she hated pink. Purple was better. Green was best. One day she'd decorate. For now, she came home, watched what *she* wanted on television, read books that she purchased with her own money, drank the occasional nice bottle of wine rather than the bottom-shelf crap that Danny used to buy, and wrote every night. But she wanted more. Companionship. Laughter. Love.

Her apartment's best feature, by far, was its proximity to a dozen bus lines. She walked to the corner, down two blocks, and hopped on the bus that would drop her next to Stanby and Associates. It wasn't the shortest ride in the world, but it was direct and she used the time to write or read. Today, she wrote in her journal.

I found him again. It was an accident. Mostly. We were supposed to go to Radiator Whiskey, but as we walked from the office, I saw the sign for Libations. Something about it called to me, though I didn't recognize what at the time. It was happy hour. Kismet, right? As it turns out, yes. I didn't recognize his logo. Not consciously. But the martini glass with the red rose inside is tattooed on his left forearm. I'd forgotten. I hadn't forgotten his accent. I don't even know where he's from, but it's got to be somewhere southern. That would explain so much of him. The chivalry. The protectiveness. Or maybe that's just what a good guy is. I've never known any.

There's something about him. I trusted him when I didn't trust myself. I have these vague memories, colored by the pain meds and the concussion, of him with me in the hospital. He held my hand. Danny never held my hand. It's the simple things that we need in life. Someone to listen. Someone to help you out of the car (not that I need it, but it's still nice), someone who says they're proud of you.

I don't know what will happen. Maybe nothing. Maybe I'm too damaged. I'm going to screw something up, screw myself up. But I can try. I'm ready to try. At least I hope I am.

After a day spent with clients, and the dual

interruptions from Jennifer and Maura asking her for details of her time with Garrett, Lilah took the bus to Safe Haven. She'd managed to wrangle a last-minute appointment with Dr. Lefterts.

"Lilah, I'm surprised to see you," Dr. Lefterts said, welcoming her into one of the private offices of the counseling center. "I thought we'd decided appointments every other week were working."

"They are. It's just . . . something happened and I need to know if I'm doing the right thing."

"No one can tell you that. We've discussed this. *You* are in control of your own life now. If you think you're doing the right thing, that has to be enough. I can only make sure you're healthy and not slipping into prior harmful behaviors. But we're getting ahead of ourselves. Let's sit and begin as we always do, with your affirmations."

Lilah took her usual place on the leather couch and closed her eyes. A few deep breaths centered her. "Dreams matter. I matter. No one can take my dreams away unless I let them."

Once she'd repeated the mantra three times, she opened her eyes.

"What are you dreaming about this week, Lilah?"

"Garrett."

Dr. Lefterts frowned, puzzled. Her head cocked to the side as she flipped through her notes. Lilah filled in the blank.

"He was there when Danny attacked me. He sat by my hospital bed that first night. Held my hand. He was the first one to tell me to leave Danny. At least the first one I listened to."

"Oh. I thought you'd lost touch with him."

"I did. But I went out for drinks with Maura and Jennifer

last night and it ended up being *his* bar. He owns it. We talked for two hours and I let him bring me home. And then I kissed him."

"And now you're wondering if it's a good idea to date him."

"Am I that transparent?" Lilah wrung her hands in her lap, the corners of her lips tugging upwards despite her best effort not to smile at the thought of a date with Garrett.

Dr. Lefterts laughed and nodded. "I'm afraid you are, but then again, we've spent a lot of time together this year talking about men and relationships. And I can't tell you whether it's a good idea or not. You said you were ready to date. You *have* dated."

"It hasn't gone well."

"No, but that's not because of you. Your last date made you feel insignificant and you walked out. That shows how much you've learned about yourself in the past year. Do you think Garrett will do that to you?"

"No. He saw me when I couldn't see myself."

"Then have fun."

"I have no fucking clue how to play golf." Garrett unloaded the dishwasher under the bar while Ro checked the liquid levels in the various bottles of scotch, vodka, rum, and shrubs.

"We're low on the peach blackberry and the cherry vanilla shrubs. And the Oban," Ro said. "And no one knows how to play golf. Not really. But dude. Ball. Club. Whack. How hard can it be?" She made a little stroking motion with an empty bottle of rye and clicked her tongue.

"I watched videos online last night. I can do just about anything any other guy can do, Ro. I'm a little slower climbing stairs, a little unsteady balancing on my bad leg. But I don't think I can play golf."

"I've never seen you insecure, boss. Hell, I didn't know you had a bum leg until you told me you had to go to the prosthetics clinic. I figured your underwear was riding up or something."

He stifled a laugh. Of course she'd think that. "No." He didn't go into any of the gory details, but he told Ro a little about the attack that had taken his leg and ended his army career. "I talked to one of my buddies last night—Mac. He's in Boston. He left Afghanistan a year ago, half dead. We lost touch for a while, but he reached out again over the holidays. He fell in love. Said it's the best thing that's ever happened to him. His woman doesn't see his scars. But . . . Lilah might see mine. It's pretty hard to miss this." He rapped on his thigh.

"She knows, right?"

Garrett nodded. "But knowin' and seein' it are two different things."

Ro jabbed him in the ribs. "Stop worrying. About all of it. If you can't play golf, do something else."

"She matters. And she wants to play golf."

Garrett's phone buzzed on the counter. *Lilah.*

"Hi, darlin'. I'm leaving in ten minutes."

Lilah's voice was strained. "Garrett, I can't do this."

"What's wrong?" He waved Ro off, ambled back to his office, and shut the door. She didn't answer, but he could hear her breathing on the other end of the line. "Lilah, talk to me. If you need to reschedule, that's fine."

"You can do better than me. I can't ask you to waste your time. Sometime soon, I'm going to freak out on you, and you'll dump me, and it's going to be harder on me to end it then than it will be if we don't start anything now."

"Who the hell says I'm goin' to dump you?"

She didn't answer.

"One date. Please, Lilah. If you feel this way tomorrow, you'll never hear from me again." He couldn't help the desperation in his tone. He'd lost her for almost a full year, and he was damn sure he wasn't going to let her go without a fight. If only he knew *how* to fight for her without compromising her independence. If it was up to him, he'd march over there right now and demand that she let him take her out. But that wouldn't work with Lilah. It would only scare her away. He'd beg if he had to.

"He screwed me up. I'm never going to be *normal*."

"Darlin', normal is boring as shit."

A choked laugh encouraged him.

"Every night, I unstrap my leg and set it next to my bed. Do you know how I clean the actual foot? Goo Gone and a toothbrush. That's not normal either. Hell, don't you think I'm terrified of you seein' my stump and runnin' away? But I'm still willin' to try. Don't let *him* come between us. Not unless you still love him."

"I never loved him."

"Then let me take you out today."

The pause on the line held his heart in a vise. He didn't know what he'd do if she said no. Probably never date again.

"Are you sure?"

He smiled. *Hell yes.* "I'll be there in twenty minutes."

Lilah answered the door before he finished knocking.

Garrett's jaw dropped. She'd pulled her strawberry-blond hair back into a ponytail and her tight jeans, baggy purple sweater, and suede boots were the picture of casual elegance. A wool coat hung over her arm and her green eyes were wide.

"Are you sure about this?" She sucked her lower lip under her teeth and chewed on it.

Garrett eased the coat from her and held it out. She turned and shrugged into the sleeves. He smoothed his hands down her arms and relished the little shiver that shook her shoulders. She turned and he offered her his arm. With her purse in one hand and his arm in the other, they walked down to his truck in silence. He wasn't going to pressure her into talking or opening up to him. Having her close was progress enough.

Halfway to the driving range, she cleared her throat. "I've been on three dates since Danny. None of them went well."

"What happened?"

She told him everything: the blind date that wanted to make out in the corner of the restaurant, the ass who assumed she couldn't make a decision for herself, and the man who might as well have been on a date with his cell phone. "None of them cared about who *I* was."

"So who are you?" Garrett asked as he opened the door for her at the driving range. "I care. Tell me about Lilah."

"I write romance novels. I like *Sherlock* and *Survivor*. I want another tattoo. And a cat. I tried every single cuisine I could think of once I got out of the hospital because I didn't honestly know what I liked. I don't care for sushi, but I love almost everything else. Except zucchini. And pine nuts. And tomatoes."

"No tomatoes?" Garrett took a step back, thumping a hand against his chest in a mock mortal wound.

"Not raw." She turned her smile to the attendant at the desk. "A bucket of balls, a three wood, a five wood, and a nine iron." The kid handed the balls to Garrett and the clubs to Lilah. She refused Garrett's offer to pay. "You can pay for dinner."

Damn right. Garrett had been raised a proper southern gentleman. He didn't like the idea of a woman paying for a thing on a date. Especially not a first date.

They found a spot on the lower level, at the end, which relieved Garrett a bit. At least no one else would see him make a fool of himself. *Just don't fall down. Whatever you do, don't twist so much you fall down.*

Lilah took a ball and set it on a white plastic tee in the middle of the AstroTurf square. "You've never played?"

"Nope."

"Put the ball a little left of center of your stance." She spread her feet a bit wider than shoulder-width apart and did a little hip wiggle to set herself. Garrett's gaze strayed to her ass, though he returned to her face when she spoke. "Don't squeeze the club too hard. I'll help you with your grip. Look down range, visualize your target."

"Kind of like shooting."

"Uh, yes."

"I had a little sniper training before I lost my leg."

Lilah exhaled slowly, drew the club back over her right shoulder, and swung through. *Plink.* The tinny sound of the club hitting the ball brought a smile to her face, and she followed through, the club coming to rest over her left shoulder. The little white ball sailed straight and true and hit the ground near the 150-yard sign.

"That's good, right?"

She smiled, a slight blush coloring her cheeks. "I was here at least twice a week over the summer." Another four balls, all within a few feet of the first, and she stepped back. "Your turn."

Garrett shoved his hands in his pockets. "I don't have to. I can watch you."

"Don't worry, stud. I'm starting you off with the nine iron. Very little torque required. Stand the way I did."

Stud. This was the Lilah he wanted to know. The confident, take charge Lilah. He moved into position and she handed him the club. It felt good in his hand. Heavy. Solid.

"Right hand first. Thumb pointing down. Left hand slides under the right. Pinky only." She wrapped her hands around his, moving his fingers, squeezing his hands when she was satisfied. She still smelled like lilacs. "Good."

He expected her to move away, but instead she leaned in and brushed a kiss against his ear. He turned his head, hoping to catch her lips, but she slipped behind him, pressing her lithe body to his back. Her pelvis rested against his ass and he stifled a groan, his cock protesting the confinement of his jeans. He was never going to be able to swing a club in this condition.

She guided his arms with her own, her embrace warmer than the heaters blasting from above. "It's from the hips, but a nine iron is a short swing. Come back with me." He twisted slightly, unwinding when she whispered, "use your left arm to pull through."

The club *thunked* against the ball, the iron having a completely different sound than the club she'd used. Though his shot only traveled fifteen feet, it was straight.

"Was that okay?" she asked, her sultry voice only inches from his ear.

He dropped the club, turned, and took her in his arms. "I want to kiss you."

"So kiss me."

Sliding his hands up her back, he held her against him, gaze locked on her mossy green eyes. A few gold flecks glowed in her irises, reflecting the overhead lights. A smudge of kohl lined her lids, offsetting her lashes. She was beautiful, so much lovelier than she'd been before, because now she wasn't afraid. "Tell me to stop and I will."

"Garrett." The tone was clear. *Quit your yammering and kiss me already.*

He backed her up against the wall of the range, caging her with his arms on her waist. Lilacs, heat, a whiff of arousal—nothing could have prepared him for how much he wanted her. Not only in his bed, but in his life. He wanted to get to know everything about this woman, the good and the bad.

Her lips parted, and a quick dart of her tongue drew his gaze. A tiny nibble along her bottom lip elicited a moan. The firm pressure of his tongue demanding access had her breathing heavily. She tasted of mint and strawberries.

She grabbed him around the waist and flipped him around, pushing him back against the wall. She stood on her tip-toes and leveled him with a smoldering stare. "We still have half a bucket of balls," she said, dropping her gaze to the bulge in his jeans. "*Your* balls are going to have to wait."

With a choked half laugh, half groan, he tipped his head back and looked to the ceiling. "God help me, darlin'. You have no idea what you're doin' to me."

"Oh, I think I do." Her smile as she turned and went back to the bucket confirmed it. Lilah McKinney had an evil streak.

~

Red Mill Burgers was a Seattle institution. Wedged into a small two-person booth with burgers, fries, and bottles of beer, Lilah couldn't quite remember the last time she had this much fun on a date—not even when she was in college. Garrett only hit half a dozen balls, most of which required her to help him, though it wasn't that he lacked the skill. No, he liked her hands on him. A slight hitch in his step when he'd gotten out of the truck had worried her, but he claimed he was fine. "Phantom pain," he said, rubbing his upper thigh. "Usually hits me when I'm hyper focused on the leg. At the gym, when I run. It'll pass."

"You run?"

"I can do anything anyone else can do." He took a swig of his beer and focused intently on the bottle when he set it down on the table.

"I didn't mean that . . . "

He pursed his lips and forced a breath. "Sorry. That wasn't fair. I was messed up for a long time after it happened. I wanted to be a fireman. I thought I could help people. Instead, I came home and needed help to get myself to and from the bathroom. My left leg was injured too. Three breaks. I've got metal pins in the femur holding it together. I was in a wheelchair for almost six months. Lived with my folks for two years. Refused to get a job, wouldn't wear the prosthetic."

"What changed?"

"A buddy of mine, Nomar, took me to get my first tattoo." He unbuttoned his cuff and rolled it up to his elbow. A red rose nestled amid bolts of lightning and dark storm clouds. On one of the lightning bolts, the words *Be Brave. Be Strong* shone like a beacon. "It wasn't my design. Nomar told me not to look until it was done. Took three hours. When I saw it, I started crying in the tattoo chair. Not my proudest moment."

"Men can't cry?" She took a sip of beer, then popped a fry into her mouth. It felt good to be here, listening, talking, with a man who saw her as a person, not a possession. He'd insisted on ordering for them, after asking her about her preferences, and had remembered her dislike of tomatoes. In four years, Danny had never once remembered she hated them.

"Sure they can cry. I had plenty of tears during rehab. Getting used to this thing"—he rapped on his thigh—"was one of the most painful things I've ever done. But I couldn't stand that I'd wasted two years of my life feeling sorry for myself. My buddy, Sam, died in that attack. I owed him more than wallowing in my parents' spare bedroom. I was supposed to protect his sister, and instead, her husband killed her while I was feeling sorry for myself. I got myself together. Went to therapy, physical and emotional, got the leg, took a job tending bar. One of my parents' friends owned a little restaurant and needed help a couple nights a week. I liked it. Shade's hired me a year later."

"Your friend's sister . . . that's how you knew." Lilah clenched her fists in her lap. That explained it. How he could be so understanding.

"Yeah. I should have done something more for her.

Even if she refused my help, I should have offered. Maybe that's why I couldn't leave you alone."

Or maybe the universe wanted us here, together, now. Lilah was a big believer in fate. In the middle of her therapy, she'd come to the realization that she didn't regret her choices in life. She'd done what she thought was right at the time. It caused her no end of pain, but she was happy now because she'd been so miserable then.

The conversation shifted, and Garrett asked Lilah how she'd learned graphic design. "I was a business major, but I always doodled and sketched in notebooks during classes. I played around with Photoshop for fun in the evenings. After I graduated, I took a job as a marketing consultant and did design work on the side until I started dating Danny. Within a year, he'd convinced me I was a shit designer. Two years and I'd quit my job because he needed help at the firm he worked for. I did the books for six months, until he fired me from that and told me to get a part time job to pay my share of the rent because his company was 'too big for me to handle.'"

Garrett stifled a growl and a muscle in his jaw ticked. Lilah reached over and squeezed his fingers. "Don't be mad. He's in jail and I'm here. With you. I don't have any regrets."

"How can you say that? He almost killed you." Garret rubbed the back of his neck, staring at her with such intensity that she wanted to look away.

"Garrett, everything we experience shapes us somehow. I hated the past four years. I cried myself to sleep more nights than not. But looking back, I couldn't have changed them. I wasn't equipped to understand what he was doing to me. By the time I hit bottom, it was too late. I couldn't get out. I had nothing. No friends, no money, no skills—or so he'd told me. I'd resigned myself to being unhappy for the rest of my life. And then I met you. You talked to me like I was worth knowing. Getting into your truck that day, Danny beating the crap out of me, getting hit by the car, all of those things combined to get me the hell out of there. I wish I'd never met him, but beyond that, no regrets."

Their dinners long gone, Garrett stood, helped her with her coat, and tucked her in the warmth of his arm. It had started to rain and they rushed out to his truck. Once the heat was on, he took her hands. "I've never met anyone I wanted to know as much as I want to know you, Lilah. I don't want to go to work tonight."

"Can I see you on Monday?"

He grinned. "Hell yes."

"Then take me home, Garrett. And kiss me before you go."

He brought her hand to his lips. "That, I can do."

chapter seven

THEY TEXTED BACK and forth on Sunday, but with Garrett's long hours at the bar and Lilah's work on her book, there wasn't a lot of time for deep conversation. They saw a movie on Monday, snuggling close in the plush seats. But movies didn't offer a lot of opportunity to talk, and what Garrett wanted to do most with Lilah, even more than getting her naked, was talk.

He kissed her good night, leaving her breathless in her doorway. She invited him in, but he shook his head, brushing his knuckles along her jaw. "Not tonight, darlin'. Tonight I want you to think of me when you fall asleep. And when you wake up. You wanted slow, you get slow. Even if it's killin' me."

By the following Saturday, after a week of phone calls, emails, and late night texts, Garrett's nerves were on overdrive. Lilah wanted him physically—she'd made that clear. The idea of her being repulsed by his leg and running kept him up at night. He was proud of his body and worked hard to keep himself in shape, but he knew he made some people uncomfortable. Men often moved away from him at the gym, staring at his prosthetic with a mix of confusion, fascination, and disgust.

Lilah threw her arms around him when he picked her

up at her apartment. "I've been looking forward to this all week." She'd curled her hair and Garrett threaded his fingers around a few tendrils, unable to look away or even move from her landing. She was the one for him. Every conversation, every laugh, every kiss told him they were meant to be. If only he could get up the courage to take her to bed. He'd never been this nervous about sex in his life, but never had it been so important to him.

"Are we going? Or do you want to stand here all day, stud? Because we have a ferry to catch."

"You're beautiful, darlin'. Took my breath away for a moment."

She blushed and tugged him towards the stairs. They didn't leave his truck during the short ferry ride to Bainbridge Island. A quick kiss turned into more: a hand on her breast, her fingers in his hair. The scent of aroused woman filled the cab of his truck. If the ride had been longer, he'd have made use of the condom he'd slipped into his wallet, just in case. But other passengers returned to their cars and they parted, reluctantly.

It was a short drive into town, and after parking, they walked hand in hand towards the little restaurant next to the theater. A car a few feet away sputtered down the road towards them and backfired. The ricochet of the sound made him jump back. He dropped her hand. He wasn't proud of the hoarse, choked curse he couldn't stifle.

"Garrett?"

Forcing air into his lungs, he bent over and rested his hands on his thighs. Black spots floated in his vision until he forced them away. "Sorry. Bad memories. They can hit when I least expect 'em. I'm fine." He straightened and wrapped his arm around her. "I should probably warn you now, though. I hate the Fourth of July. Sounds too much like enemy fire. Even eight years later, it's still kind of hard for me."

The dark corner booth in the intimate restaurant along with Lilah's occasional comforting hand on his thigh throughout lunch quickly banished the flashback from his mind. Lilah laughed so hard she cried at the comedy show, but on the ferry ride back, all joy drained from her eyes. She pulled him to the back of the boat, ducked into a booth, and pressed herself against the window, shaking.

"What's wrong?"

"One of Danny's buddies. Hank. I don't think he saw me."

Garrett sat up a little straighter, every protective instinct on overdrive. No one was going to hurt Lilah. Not when he was around. "Where?"

"Leave it alone, Garrett. I'll be okay. I just don't want to see him. He sat behind Danny during the trial and he screamed at me one day outside the courtroom. He's harmless, but mean."

Garrett wanted to hold her, but she huddled deeper into her jacket and drew her knees up to her chest. Her heels balanced on the bench. They passed the rest of the ferry ride in silence. Garrett was at a loss for anything to say to make her feel better. He scanned the passengers religiously, looking for anyone paying undue attention to Lilah, but no one stood out. He took her down to the truck early, letting her curl against him with her eyes closed. At least she let him hold her in the safety of his cab.

When they reached her door, she pulled away before he could kiss her. "I'm sorry I ruined our day."

"You ruined nothing, darlin'. Do you want me to stay

with you? I could call Ro. Sleep on the couch. Nothin' needs to happen."

"No. I need to write. It helps. And I need to deal with this alone." She took a deep, shuddering breath. "Good night, Garrett."

"Lilah, please."

"Good night." She stifled a little sob and slipped inside her apartment. The thunk of the lock resonated in him like a physical blow to the stomach.

I have bad days. Triggers. He knew triggers. Hell, he'd had one this afternoon. That one had been minor, but he'd witnessed a serious car accident a couple of years ago and the sound of metal against metal and the scent of burning rubber had brought him back to Iraq. He'd found himself on the ground outside his truck, rocking back and forth and praying rather than calling the cops. He wasn't proud of losing his shit like that, but it wasn't something he could control.

Before he left Lilah's apartment complex, he sent her a single text.

I'm here for you. Whatever you need.

She didn't reply and Garrett's heart ached.

Monday was a bust. Stanby sent Lilah to Portland to meet with a client and the train didn't bring her back to Seattle until well after ten p.m. At least she called him and asked if he'd pick her up. She was breathlessly excited about the work and Saturday seemed to be long forgotten.

"If this goes well, I'll be eligible for a promotion," she said, grinning from ear to ear. "I'd lead a small team of designers. A year ago, I wouldn't even doodle on napkins and now I'm close to running a department."

"That's fantastic, Lilah." He turned off 175th, heading towards Kenmore. He wanted to talk about what had happened on Saturday, but he wouldn't do anything that would ruin her good mood. Not now.

"But it means I can't see you next Monday either." She cringed, looking over at him from under lowered lashes. "I'm sorry."

"Am I supposed to be mad?" He reached over and stroked her thigh, and was relieved when she didn't pull away. "I'm not *him*, darlin'. I want to see you whenever I can, but I can be patient. And there's still this Saturday. How 'bout I take the whole night off so we can have a proper date? Dinner, maybe drinks at Zig Zag? We could even go dancin' if you want. I can't promise to be good at it, but I'd try."

"I'd like that," she said, relaxing against the seat. "I'm sorry I freaked out. You don't deserve that. It wasn't like I even had to deal with Hank, but . . . I don't want you to see me like I used to be. I'm not proud of that person."

Garrett's hands tightened on the steering wheel. There was so much he wanted to say to her, but this was dangerous territory. He had to make her understand without coming across as overbearing or controlling. With a few deep breaths, he turned into her apartment complex parking lot and cut the engine. "We're together, aren't we?"

"Y-yes." A shy smile tugged at her lips. "I care about you. Spending time with you makes me happy. We're together."

"Then one of these days, we're goin' to see each other at our worsts. That's what happens in a relationship. I can deal, darlin'. All I'll ever ask is that you don't hide from me." Garrett pulled her against him, pressing a kiss to her temple. "I've got my own demons."

"I don't want to say good night. Come up with me?"

If only it wasn't so late. "I've got a meeting at the city planner's office at nine to get a permit for outdoor seating. You have to go to work in the morning. I want to do this right, Lilah. Us. If I come in, do you think I'd leave tonight?"

A blush colored her cheeks. She wore a felted gray winter hat, and when she looked down, it hid her eyes. "No."

Tipping her chin up, he searched her face. He'd worried every day that she didn't feel the same way as he did about their relationship. He liked her. Thought he might be edging towards love. But before things got any more serious, she had to see him without his leg. And that . . . that might be more than she could handle. He wasn't proud of the fear that sat like a stone in his gut, nor the roughness to his voice when he spoke again. "I miss you every day I don't get to see you. This is going to be the longest week of my life. But I promise you one thing. I will make Saturday worth the wait."

She leaned in and kissed him, capturing his bottom lip with her teeth, and then pulled away slowly, teasing him with the promise of more. "I'm counting on it."

On Tuesday, rain and wind knocked down power lines in the north end of town, felled trees along Lake Washington, and left the bar largely empty. So when the door opened at six, Garrett did a double-take. "Lilah?"

Her smile, so wide and happy, clashed with the rest of her appearance. She was soaked. Mascara smudged around her eyes, her black tights were splattered with mud, and water sheeted off her rain coat. She pulled off her hat, shook it outside the door, and then made a beeline for the bar.

"I missed you."

He cupped the back of her head, drew her against him, and kissed her for all he was worth. Two patrons stood and applauded when he was done and Lilah blushed.

"Garrett," she admonished, "not in public."

"I don't care, darlin'. I'm not ashamed of kissin' my girlfriend in my own bar. But I am sorry if I embarrassed you. Come back to my office. I've got a dry shirt back there. Your raincoat didn't do much for you."

With her chilled hand in his, he nodded to his server, Helen, and headed for the hall. Once inside his private space, he shut the door, backed her up against it, and framed her face with his hands. He couldn't help his grin. "I love seein' you in my bar." This kiss was tender, his tongue dancing with hers as he nibbled her lower lip, but his dick throbbed against his jeans. If their relationship was further along, he'd take her on the desk, but he wanted to make their first time special. Romantic. Memorable. Though he supposed sex on his desk *would* be memorable. He chuckled.

"What's so funny?" she asked, narrowing her eyes at him.

He tried to deflect, but she took him by the shoulders and pushed him back a couple of steps. "Spill it, stud."

"I was thinkin' how I wanted to make Saturday night special."

"Uh-huh." Her gaze fell to his jeans. "Special."

Caught in his lie, Garrett spun around and dug a black, long sleeved shirt out of his bottom desk drawer that would probably dwarf her. He always kept a couple spare shirts in his office. He tried to put on a little bit of a show for his customers and that occasionally resulted in spilled mixers. He passed her the shirt, along with a spare bar towel. "I'll make you a hot toddy?"

"I'd like that."

Behind the bar, he mixed up his own personal recipe: chamomile tea, whiskey, mead, and his signature twist—a shot of peach liqueur.

Lilah took a seat at the corner of the bar, his shirt looking much better on her than it ever had on him. Cupping the mug, she inhaled deeply. "I hope you don't mind that I came."

"You're welcome here any day of the week, darlin'. My only regret is that I can't take you home. Ro's off tonight and my backup bartender is sick." He wiped down part of the bar in front of her, keeping half an eye on the other five patrons in Libations. He'd love to close up shop early, drive her home, and spend the rest of the night with her. Saturday couldn't come quick enough.

"I can't stay long anyway. I've got to get a few chapters of my next book out to my editor tonight. But I couldn't face an entire night of proofreading after a full day of meetings without something good in between."

"Well, then let me get you something to eat. Do you trust me?"

Her smile answered his question.

They talked every day that week: stolen conversations

while he was on break in his office, text messages on her lunch hour, emails where she shared bits of her next book. He'd bought her first one, a heartbreakingly accurate story of an abused woman who escaped her husband, only to find herself on the run. It had been cathartic to write, she'd said, and her next book was more of a lighter story of redemption. He understood what she needed—from him and from herself—and he hoped this weekend would mark a serious turn in their relationship.

He couldn't recall ever being this nervous as he rubbed some sandalwood-scented oil over his stubble. Lilah had affectionately called him scruffy once, and though she seemed to like the hair that darkened his upper lip, jaw, and chin, he took extra care with his appearance today. He wasn't planning on ending the night alone.

Naked, he cleaned his prosthetic and allowed his mind wander. His right leg ended nine inches below his hip. Though he had minimal scarring—his surgeon had been a miracle worker—the sight of his stump, when it wasn't hidden by the compression sleeve he wore to help secure it to the socket, wasn't for the faint of heart. He had to admit, it was why he'd gone a little overboard on the tattoos. Not only did they cover his arms from wrist to shoulder, they also enveloped his chest, down both sides of his ribcage. He'd adorned his left leg with a proud green, red, and black dragon, whose tail curled at his ankle and mouth angled towards his cock.

Once he'd slid his leg into the socket, tightened the mechanism that held it in place, and tested the fit, he donned a pair of black slacks, a long sleeved maroon shirt, gray vest, and a pair of Doc Martens. He grabbed a small backpack and tossed in a fresh pair of underwear, a spare compression sleeve, and a toothbrush. He didn't know whether they'd return to his place or go to hers, but if she was willing, they were going to end this date with breakfast in the morning and he wanted to be prepared.

They shared half a dozen small plates at dinner in Pioneer Square, interspersing eating with holding hands. Many moments fueled his desire for her: lingering touches over the bread knife, Lilah's delight when the host—who'd tried to hire Garrett away from Shade's more than once—sent over glasses of champagne with his compliments, and the intensity with which she devoured her chocolate mousse.

Afterward, they walked up to Pike Street. Zig Zag was crowded enough that they had to wait outside the door for a table. Garrett held her close, both for warmth and to steal a few precious minutes with his hands on her ass. He groaned when she snuggled closer. She turned her green-eyed gaze up to him. "Are you okay?"

He was already semi-hard. Oh, who was he kidding, he'd been aching for her all night. Terrified, but very aroused. "You're makin' it hard to romance you, darlin'."

"Take me home, Garrett."

"You're not having fun?" Panic stabbed at him. He'd said something wrong. Something that triggered her. Except, she was smiling. And pressing her hips against him.

"Your home. Take me back to your place."

He couldn't get her to the truck fast enough.

~

Garrett lived in an apartment complex at the edge of downtown. It was small, but his top-floor unit had a view of Puget Sound. He unlocked his door and let her enter. Thank God he'd cleaned up the night before. And bought that box of condoms. *What if she bolts?* He'd only shown his leg to three women outside of the nurses in the hospital and the physical therapists. Two had run almost immediately. The other—Debra—hadn't minded it, but she'd asked him to keep his compression sleeve on while they fucked.

A brown leather couch, coffee table, and flat screen television dominated the small living room. Beyond that, the kitchen was small, but functional, especially for a bachelor who could only make a dozen dishes. His bedroom and bath were off to the left, and he hoped he'd put the seat down. No woman wanted to walk in on that. He knew he'd left a few pieces of his prosthetic in the corner of his bedroom. He had a bigger spare foot for running, tools he could use to tighten things if he needed to, and the cleaning products he used every day.

She toured the small space, looking at the photos of his buddies in Iraq and his parents in front of their retirement home in Hawaii. His collection of DVDs and the cocktail reference books littered his coffee table and bookshelves. He fucking loved seeing her in his space and from the expression on her face, she didn't mind it too much either.

Please don't let her run.

"Have a seat." He wasn't proud of the roughness in his voice or the uncomfortable throbbing against his zipper. He wanted her, but was she ready for this?

"I don't want to sit."

Garrett dropped his keys, missing the counter completely in his haste to get to Lilah. His hands framed her face, tangling in her hair. Stumbling towards the bedroom, he moved by feel, his eyes locked on hers. "I've wanted to do this since the first time I touched you," he said, savoring the taste of her, the scent of lilacs on her skin, and the silky strands of her hair. He wanted to lose himself in her.

Lilah tugged his vest up and he took a step back, letting her pull it off. She tossed it in the corner of the room. Pushing him down onto the bed, she straddled him and unbuttoned his shirt. The lightning bolts over his heart formed the stems of half a dozen roses in front of a tombstone. The names of his dead platoon mates adorned the stone. Tears formed a pool on his left ribs, around which he'd added a new phrase. *Dreams don't die.*

"When did you get this?" Her eyes narrowed at the familiar phrase.

"After I left you in the hospital. I wanted something to remember you by."

"Garrett, I want you to tell me the story behind every one of these. Later. Take off your pants."

This wasn't the Lilah he'd met a year ago. This wasn't the scared girl he'd rescued. This was *Lilah*. His Lilah. "Are you sure?"

"I wouldn't have come here if I wasn't. I like you. A lot. I feel like I could love you one day." She stroked the resin under his pants. "I don't care about this. I know you think I should, but I don't." She shed her sweater. Pink scars zigzagged across her abdomen, long healed, but still quite visible.

Garrett sat up, bringing her with him. "What happened?" He couldn't help his growl. If that fucking asshole had done this to her . . .

"I was stabbed in an alley. Four years ago. Mugging gone wrong. I was twenty weeks pregnant. Danny and I hadn't been careful with contraception. It's what initially kept us together. The baby." She pressed her lips together for a long minute. "My daughter died and I'll never be able to have children. I blamed myself, thought my scars were a fitting punishment. Maybe I thought Danny was a punishment too. It took me a long time to forgive myself for cutting through that alley. I don't think I did until this past year. That's when I really started to heal. We all have scars. We're all missing parts of ourselves." Then, pressing a flat hand to his tattooed chest, she lowered her voice. "Take off your pants. Let me see you."

He needed a minute. Winding his arms around her, he pulled her against his bare chest, relishing the feel of her skin, her hot breath against his neck, and the kisses she feathered from his shoulder to his ear. "I'm scared, darlin'."

"Don't be." Lilah wriggled out of his arms and settled back against his pillows. Her black lace bra did nothing to hide the hard points of her nipples. He raked his gaze over her stomach. The jagged scars were a part of her, and though he saw them, they did nothing to diminish her beauty. No, they added to it. She knew loss and pain. That's what she'd meant about no regrets. He reached out, traced one of the lines along her soft skin. Lilah was beautiful, imperfections and all. He'd never look at his leg the same way again.

She kicked off her heels and licked her lips. God, he wanted her.

His shoes came off first, then his socks. She looked down at his right foot, her head slightly cocked, but she was otherwise nonplussed by the flesh-toned resin. His hands shook as he unbuckled his belt and lowered his zipper. Fabric rustled, his pants hit the floor, and he stepped out of them, terrified. Her gaze went first to the dragon that peeked out of his black boxer briefs. She leaned forward and traced its scales, down his left leg, around his knee. A shiver ran along his spine. After kissing the dragon's head, she turned her attention to his *other* leg. The white compression sleeve covered his upper thigh. The dark maroon resin socket, embellished with a similar dragon, done in green and gold, ended at his knee joint where titanium took over.

"May I?" Her hands hovered at his hips.

"Yeah."

Nothing prepared him for how good it felt to have her hands on him. Her fingers trailed down his hips to the prosthetic. She smoothed her fingers around his socket, a shy smile tugging at her lips. She didn't stop there. Caressing every bit of his leg, the charger that controlled the movement of his calf and ankle, down to his foot, and back up again, she touched the sleeve that protected his stump. "Did you think I'd run?"

"Most people do."

"I'm not most people." His leg now forgotten, she rose up to her knees, continuing the exploration of his body. The tree along his right ribs earned a kiss. "I love this. The strength behind it." Her fingers stroked the *v* that angled into his boxers and she feathered a light touch over his dick, rock hard and throbbing.

That was enough. Garrett grabbed her behind her knees and tugged her forward on the bed. She fell back, laughing. He unzipped her long skirt, and it joined his vest across the room. She was so damn sexy in her black lace panties and bra—sexier when she pulled down one of the bra straps to reveal a breast and pert nipple. "God, Lilah. I've dreamed about this."

"Then stop gawking and get down here, stud."

She didn't need to ask him twice. Climbing onto the bed, he covered her body with his and kissed her. Heat built between them, her arousal as sweet as rain, his cock straining against the fabric of his boxer briefs. She reached between them, sliding her fingers under his waistband and around his erection. He groaned, the pleasure overwhelming. It had been so long since he'd felt another woman's touch. Lilah was everything he wanted. Someone who knew pain and had come out the other side.

Her fingernails scraped against his inner thigh, eliciting a shudder that ran up and down his body.

"It's been a long time," she whispered. "Tell me if I do something wrong."

"You're doin' just fine, darlin'. But you're going to have to hang on. I want to taste you."

Her breath caught in her throat and she moaned when he pressed his hand against her lace-covered mound. "Garrett?"

"What?" He grinned, tugging down her panties. A trim triangle of curls glistened with dew. One finger dipped inside her and she pressed her hips against him. He kissed a trail down her stomach, swirling his tongue around her navel, and nuzzled her curls.

"What are you doing?"

"Going down on you. What did you think I was doing?"

"I've never . . . "

Garrett lifted himself up on his elbows. "You've got to be kidding . . . "

She shook her head and he chuckled.

"Oh, darlin', we're goin' to have some fun tonight."

Her thighs trembled under his touch. The sweet scent of lilacs filled his nose. "Do you trust me?"

"Y-yes."

His first taste of her essence exploded on his tongue: sweet and almost floral. The nub of her sex throbbed under his attention, and Lilah's gasps and moans drove him on. She twisted her hands in the sheets, begging him for more.

"Garrett!" Her final cry as she tumbled over the edge was hoarse with need. After he sated himself with her taste, he crawled up to gather her in his arms.

A tear trailed down her cheek, landing with a plop on his chest and panic shot through him. "What's wrong, darlin'? Did I do somethin'?"

"No." Lilah shuddered with the aftermath of her orgasm, sighing and snuggling closer. "That was . . . amazing."

"Amazing, huh?"

She turned her gaze up to meet his and grinned. "Yes. Now, it's your turn."

Sliding off the bed, he pulled off his boxers. Lilah's green-eyed gaze focused on his cock standing proudly, heavy and hard for her.

"I want to touch you." She crawled forward, wrapping gentle fingers around his length.

He groaned, pushed into her touch, and tangled his hands in her hair. "Lie back, darlin'." He snagged a condom from his nightstand and tore into the foil. Sheathed, he knelt on the bed and spread her thighs. "I've dreamed about this. Every single night since I found you in my bar." Locking his gaze with hers, he pushed into her, taking his time so she could get used to his length.

Her breasts heaved with her pants and cries as he thrust, and when he reached down to pinch her nipple, her second orgasm took her. A breath later, he let himself follow.

~

Lilah snuggled against Garrett's chest. He'd drawn the blankets over her naked body and rested his arm along her lower back. His prosthetic leg stuck out of the sheets.

"Do you, uh, take it off?" She stroked her hand down his hip, touching the compression sleeve.

"Every night. Can't sleep in it."

"What about . . . getting up, going to the bathroom?"

"There are crutches under the bed. It's easier than getting in and out of the leg. Unless I want to hop. Which can be dangerous in the middle of the night. Or after drinkin'."

She laughed, sitting up and pulling the covers up to her breasts. "I want to see all of you."

Garrett fiddled with the resin socket at the top of his thigh. After a moment, a faint suction sound met her ears. He wiggled the leg off to reveal a stump only a little over half the length of his left thigh and a fair bit thinner. With a look to her for approval, he rolled down the compression sleeve.

Lilah stroked her hand over the top of his thigh. "Does it hurt?"

"No. I get phantom pain. My calf hurts sometimes. My knee. But not as much as it used to." He shifted closer to her, intertwining their fingers. "You're not runnin'."

A wave of sadness washed over her. He really expected her to leave him when she saw his leg. There was nowhere else in the world she'd rather be. *Well, in his arms might be better.* "No. I'm staying right here. All night if you'll have me."

"It's been a long time since I had a woman in my bed,

darlin'. I wasn't lookin' forward to you leavin'. Come here."

For the first time in many years, Lilah fell asleep in a man's arms, cherished, sated, and happy.

The metallic click of crutches woke her. A few minutes later, Garrett opened the bathroom door, spilling a crack of light over Lilah's face. They locked gazes. "Shit." Garrett was naked, balancing on his good leg as he reached for the light switch.

"It's okay. I'm a light sleeper. You spend enough time on crutches, you never forget that sound." She patted the bed. He moved quickly. After shutting off the light, he made his way back to her in a dozen steps and stowed his crutches under the bed.

Garrett pulled the blankets over them, bringing his rich bourbon and leather scent to her nose. Snuggling closer to him, she felt his erection jutting firmly against her hip. "Well, we *are* both awake," she murmured, trailing her fingers over his chest. She pinched his nipple and was rewarded by a groan.

The drawer of his nightstand rattled and the foil packet tore in his hands. "You've got to be on top, darlin'."

Of course. He couldn't kneel over her without his prosthetic. She straddled him, easing herself down over his length. With her hands on his chest, she rolled her hips back and forth, enjoying being in control. His groans and grunts spurred her on. He circled her wrists with strong fingers, holding her in place.

"Faster."

She complied, squeezing him, throwing her head back

when he tightened his grip and jerked, shouting her name. Collapsing against him, she relished his strong arms around her, and stifled her moan when he pulled out and tossed the condom into the wastebasket at the side of the bed.

"Your turn."

"What?" Shocked, she sat up.

"Sex isn't all about me, darlin'. If anything, it's all about you."

"I came. Earlier."

"You did. Twice. I like the number three."

chapter eight

WAKING UP IN Garrett's bed with the scent of their lovemaking all around them wasn't the calm, reassuring experience Lilah had imagined. Insecurities abounded, and she sat up, staring at his face relaxed with sleep. His naked chest, covered in ink, rose and fell steadily. Her feelings for him had grown by leaps and bounds the previous night, fueled by the intensity of the physical connection between them.

Lilah wasn't a prude, or an ingénue, but she'd never slept naked, never made love twice in one night, and never laughed in the middle of sex. Garrett alternated between serious and playful, but his focus had always been completely on her. *Sex isn't all about me, darlin'. If anything, it's all about you.*

"You're starin'," he said, not bothering to open his eyes. "And thinkin' so hard I can hear you."

"Can I borrow a shirt?"

He blinked, focusing on her face, and then trailed his gaze down to the sheet clutched to her chest. "Top drawer."

Lilah scrambled for the dresser, wishing she could have taken the sheet with her. Garrett watched her, his hands folded behind his head. She found a dark blue Mariners

T-shirt and tugged it over her head. It fell to mid-thigh. Covered, and thus reassured slightly, she turned back to him. What would he expect now? "Can I make you breakfast or something?"

"You're not my maid, Lilah. Come back to bed. It's Sunday. I don't have anywhere to be."

"Coffee, then." She didn't want to get back in bed. *In bed* meant she had to talk to him, let him in. All the way in.

"Beans are in the cabinet to the left of the sink. Two scoops, the machine does the rest." Garrett sat up, grabbed his crutches, and headed for the bathroom. The click of the door made Lilah flinch. He wasn't happy with her, but he hadn't raised his voice at all. She wasn't sure what to do with that. Other than make coffee.

When she returned with two mugs, he was back in bed wearing a pair of flannel pajama pants and a black T-shirt. His elbow rested on his knee. "We're going to get something out of the way, right now," he said, accepting the mug. "There's only one thing I'll ever demand from you. Don't run away from me like you just did."

"I didn't—"

"You did. You were scared and you ran to the kitchen, hoping you could deflect by doing somethin' you thought I wanted. I don't want you to cook or clean or pretend to be someone you're not. I want you to talk to me. I'm fallin' for you, Lilah. Hard. I hope you're fallin' for me too. But this can't work if you don't let me in."

A tear burned in her eye. Of all the things he could have said, that wasn't what she expected, but it was everything she wanted. "Guys like you don't exist."

"I exist."

Oh, did he. All six-foot-two inches of tattooed soldier

who'd made her come three times the previous night. She got back in bed, clutching her coffee mug to her chest like a shield. "Pillow talk isn't something I'm good at."

"There's a pillow," he said, nodding. "You're talking. Seems to me you're doin' just fine."

"Funny man."

"Tell me what scares you."

Lilah inhaled sharply. "This. This is what I'm not good at."

"I want to know everything about you, Lilah. Why you stayed with him, why you left, what I can do to make you happy." He drained his mug, settled back against the pillows, and waited.

"I don't trust myself most of the time. That's what scares me. I hate that I didn't see what Danny was doing to me until he'd reduced me to . . . nothing."

"You were never nothin', Lilah. Never."

She set her mug down on the bedside table, took hold of the blanket, and twisted it in her hands. "I was. You're nothing when you *think* you're nothing. I'm someone now. I'm a writer, a designer, a book lover. I can sing a little. I like to run and play golf and watch old movies. I matter. Today. But what happens tomorrow?"

Lilah gave up trying to be strong and curled into Garrett's chest. He smelled like her, along with leather, sex, and bourbon. "I wake up every day and look in the mirror and tell myself that I matter. That my dreams are important. All of them. When I was with Danny, my only dreams were his dreams. I didn't have any of my own. I used to cry myself to sleep at night wishing, hoping that one day he'd ask me what I wanted. Or that he'd take an interest in something I enjoyed. Or that he'd love me. But he never did. We never said the words."

Garrett tightened his arms around her. "Why did you stay?"

"At first, the baby. After I was stabbed, I spent a week in the hospital. When I got out, Danny took care of me. He did everything for me. Helped me to the bathroom, changed my bandages. Everything. That's part of why I stayed. We had this shared . . . thing. He was sweet. Tender. At that point, I thought maybe one day I'd love him."

"It's okay if you did," Garrett said, his voice quiet against her ear.

Neither of them spoke for what felt like forever. Garrett laid his hand against her belly and Lilah broke. The walls around her heart crumbled into dust with that single touch. She didn't cry. She didn't have any tears left for her daughter or for the innocence she'd never get back. She didn't even have any tears left for her relationship with Danny. All she had was the truth. "I didn't. Love requires respect. Reciprocity. Caring. You can't be in a loving relationship when one partner is disgusted by the other. Danny never had sex with me with the lights on again unless he took me from behind. He hated looking at me. I don't know if I reminded him of our daughter and what he'd lost or if he was just a shallow, manipulative bastard who wanted a trophy wife and ended up with me because some misplaced sense of guilt kept him there. Either way, he made my life hell and I let him."

Garrett flinched. "I really wish I'd been able to leave a few permanent marks on that bastard."

"You did enough, Garrett. More. You saved my life."

"Barely."

Lilah trailed her knuckles along the rough stubble of his jaw. "No, you did more than stop him from hitting me.

You were the first person in a long time who talked to me like I was worth knowing." She straddled him, locking her legs around his torso. "I'm falling for you too. Now what are we doing for breakfast? I'm hungry."

chapter nine

LILAH SPENT THE following Friday night perched on a stool in Libations. Garrett moved behind the bar with ease, chatting with customers and dropping off sparkling glasses of various non-alcoholic shrubs for her. Fruit-based concoctions mixed with soda water tickled Lilah's throat and complemented the small plates of bacon-wrapped dates, cheeses, and cured meats. Spending time with Garrett, in his element—even if he could only spare a few moments for a stolen kiss, a smile, or a caress—was the highlight of her week. Even more of a highlight than the promotion she'd received a few hours ago. He'd promised to celebrate with her after closing, and they were headed to Portland in the morning for a romantic weekend. Three weeks together and she was close to confessing her love for him, despite the insecurities that plagued her from time to time. Dr. Lefterts assured her that what she felt was normal. Battered women rarely admitted their own worth, and though Lilah knew Garrett cared deeply for her, she still found herself in that dark cave of self-doubt when they weren't together. Valentine's Day was approaching, and she didn't know how she was going to handle being in love (or close to it) on that holiday.

Ro took a break and leaned against the back wall of the bar, sipping a tall glass of water. "He's changed," she said, nodding towards Garrett. "There's something lighter about him now. Happier. He said you met when you were dating someone else."

Lilah's cheeks flamed and she stared into her drink. "I was. And then that someone beat the shit out of me."

"Told me that too. What happened to the asswipe?" Ro leaned closer. She had a tattoo of a snake around her left arm and a lion on her right. Lilah admired the woman. She was short—barely five foot three—but she packed a punch of personality in that little body. In the few evenings Lilah had spent at the bar, she'd seen Ro handle several assholes who'd tried to hit on her and one drunk who'd reminded her of Danny.

Ro cleared her throat, bringing Lilah back.

"He's in jail."

Ro nodded. "Gotcha. Where are you and Garrett going tomorrow?"

"Portland. I got a promotion—"

"Fucking bitch!" A strong arm hauled Lilah off the stool and threw her against the wall. Her shoulder sang from the impact. She threw her hands up, fending off a hard slap that glanced off her forearm. Hank's dark eyes and thin mouth curled into a snarl. "You ruined his life."

"Lilah!" Garrett flew towards her. Before he got to Hank, Lilah brought her knee up and rammed Hank's groin. The brute screamed and clutched his balls, twisting and falling to his knees.

"He almost killed me," Lilah spat, "so shut the fuck up about what *I* did. He ruined his own goddamn life."

Garrett pulled Lilah behind him and glared at the writhing man on the floor. "Call the cops, Ro."

"No." Lilah touched Garrett's arm. "Kick him out, but I don't want to press charges. I want him gone."

He turned and cupped her cheek. "He hurt you."

"I hurt him too."

Garrett grinned, nodding. "Yes, you did. Fine." He faced Hank. The man had gotten to his feet, but he was still cupping his balls. "Get the fuck out of here. If I see you again, I'm callin' the police. And don't even *think* about coming after Lilah. I've got a dozen witnesses in here that saw you attack her."

"Fucking cripple," Hank spat. "Danny shoulda messed you up a hell of a lot more than he did."

As soon as the door closed, Lilah sagged against Garrett, shaking. "I need to sit down."

He walked her back to his office and got her a bottle of water from his mini fridge. "I'm going to call in my other bartender. He's a hulk and he'll make sure there's no more trouble. Then we're leaving. Your place or mine, I don't care, but I don't want you to be alone tonight."

Lilah nodded. She wasn't sure she wanted to be alone either. A blanket, a bed, and Garrett's arms around her sounded pretty damn good right now.

Garrett turned and was almost out of the room when Hank's words sunk in. "What did he mean?" she asked, grabbing Garrett's arm. "When he said Danny messed you up?"

Garrett grimaced and rubbed the top of his right leg. "The day he tried to kill you, he did some damage to my prosthetic. Most of it's damn near indestructible, but a couple of the mechanisms are sensitive. Gettin' it fixed took some time."

"How did he even know?"

"I testified to it at the bastard's trial."

~

Garrett's phone rang a little after midnight. Lilah jerked awake, stumbled over to his pants, and fished out the phone. The sound had woken Garrett as well. He sat up with a grunt and accepted the phone.

"Yeah?" There was a pause. "Shit. Is she okay?"

Lilah didn't know what was going on, but Garrett threw the covers off and swung his leg over the side of the bed, clearly intending to get up. "I'll be there in twenty minutes. Thanks, Bill."

He tossed the phone aside and pulled on his compression sleeve. "Hank and one of his buddies broke down the door of Libations. Ro and Bill were still inside, doing inventory. The place is mostly fine, but the shitstain dislocated her shoulder. She's in the hospital. Nothing broken, but it could have been bad if she'd been alone."

Lilah sank down to the floor, shaking, wishing she'd taken that Xanax she'd contemplated earlier. It was all because of her. Ro could have been seriously hurt. *Garrett* could have been there. Any other night and he'd have been the one closing up.

"Lilah, I need to go talk to the cops and get to the hospital to see Ro. I want you to come with me. Please." He secured his prosthetic and pulled on his pants. "Lilah? Shit, darlin'." He bent down, took her by the arms, and lifted her to her feet. She tried to pull away, but he held tight. "Look at me."

The heat from his bare chest seeped into her skin through her sleep shirt. Why did Hank have to ruin things? And how had he even found her at Libations in the first place? It had to have been when she had coffee with one of

Danny's former bosses two days ago. Hank still worked at Danny's old firm. *Oh God.* He might know where she lived. "It's my fault," she whispered. "Ro. The bar. It's all my fault."

"No. Hank is going to jail. Then it'll be done. Libations is doing well enough. We can beef up our security system, make sure this all blows over. You are *not* going to blame yourself. Get dressed. I'm not leavin' you here alone."

Lilah dressed on autopilot. Garrett got her keys, locked her door, and helped her into his truck. She couldn't stop shaking, even when he turned the heat up to maximum. More than once Garrett reached over and squeezed her hand, touched her thigh, or told her it was going to be okay, but she wasn't sure she believed him anymore. The strength she'd carefully cultivated and nurtured over the past year deteriorated with every passing minute. Why couldn't Danny and his friends leave her alone? She'd put him in jail and even now, couldn't escape him.

"Lilah? Come on, darlin'. Inside now." Garrett opened the passenger-side door and took her arm. She jerked, a hoarse sob escaping before she got herself under control. Wide green eyes took in the scene: two police cars with their lights flashing, three officers, and Bill—Garrett's fill-in bartender. The splintered front door of the bar dangled from a hinge. One of the closest tables to the door was overturned; the leg was broken off and abandoned a few feet away.

"Ro went to the hospital," Bill said. "Cops are searching for the guys."

Garrett turned to one of the officers, the one writing in a small notebook. "Can we go inside? It's cold out here."

"We've got the crime scene techs on the way. Until we get things printed, it's not a good idea."

Bill cleared his throat. "I've got a blanket in my car, boss."

"Get it."

Once Lilah was wrapped in a red wool blanket and back in the cab of Garrett's truck, he spent half an hour talking to the police. He gave them a detailed statement about the earlier trouble and Lilah's history with Danny Brogan. One of the officers made a few calls and talked to the detective who'd taken Lilah's report in the hospital. Garrett had security cameras that caught the break-in and the case was, in the officer's words, "a slam dunk." Their only concern was finding the guys. Lilah supplied the names and the addresses she knew from the previous year: Hank Bridle, his brother Larry Bridle, and Danny's former college roommate Benji Yalen. No one knew who the second man was, but Lilah maintained that it had to be one of those other two.

Bill left to check on Ro. Once the crime scene tech had printed the door and broken table, Garrett brought Lilah inside, made her a hot toddy, and took her upstairs where she could curl up next to the fire. She'd barely spoken, other than to the police, and Garrett was worried.

Between securing the broken front door and leaving messages for the alarm company and his insurance agent, he was tired, angry, and sore by the time he trudged back upstairs to check on her. Lilah's eyes were closed, but the rest of her body hid underneath the blanket.

"Darlin'. Wake up." Garrett touched her shoulder and she yelped.

"Don't, Danny!" She burrowed further under the blanket, shaking.

"No, Lilah. It's Garrett. Look at me." He didn't touch her, but dropped down to his good knee a foot away. "It's Garrett."

She launched herself at him, knocking him off his feet and onto his ass. He didn't care. He'd skid down a flight of stairs if it'd take that panic out of her voice. "Shh, it's okay." He rubbed her back as her tears soaked his shirt. "Let it out. I'm here."

"Sorry," she said, loud hiccups taking place of her sobs. "Haven't had . . . a nightmare . . . in a while."

"Don't apologize. It's been a fucking awful night. And it's not over." He smoothed a hand over her cheek, tucking a few locks of hair behind her ear. "We need to go to the hospital now. Bill called. They're waitin' on x-rays. I don't want Ro to be by herself. Can you hang on a little longer for me?"

Lilah nodded, getting to her feet and offering him her hand. His pride didn't want to take the help, but his aching body won the argument. He limped more than he liked going down the stairs. Checking to make sure that asswipe Brogan didn't have any more *friends*, he led Lilah to his truck.

~

"She's okay, boss. They're going to release her as soon as they fit her with a sling." Bill sat in a hard plastic chair in the ER waiting room, looking the worse for wear. His knuckles were bandaged and the bright waiting room lights revealed a dark red stain on his gray pants.

"Thank God." Garrett's gaze zeroed in on a coffee machine in the corner. He really should have made a pot at the bar. He tipped a few coins into the machine, punched the button for black, and waited as the machine spewed a bitter brew into a small cup. "Either of you want one?"

Bill shook his head. "I've had three already. I'm good. That shit'll wear a hole in your gut."

"Once you've had the motor oil they serve in the mess, nothing bothers you. I doubt I'm goin' to be sleepin' tonight. I need the kick. Lilah?"

"No, thank you." The formality of her tone worried him. She sat quietly, hands folded in her lap. Her green eyes had lost their usual luster and her shoulders slumped.

Garrett took a seat next to her, his palm upturned on his thigh. He hoped she'd take it, but she stared at the floor, barely moving. The trio waited in silence for half an hour until a nurse came out, dressed in pink scrubs. Her bouncy curls were barely tamed by a headband.

"I'm looking for a Bill Phillips?"

"That's me." Bill stood, hands in his pockets.

Garrett stood too. "We're with Ro Wexley. All three of us."

The nurse cracked a smile. "Gotcha. You can see her now. She's going to be discharged shortly. Follow me."

Ro sat in the center of a hospital bed, legs crossed under a blanket and left arm in a sling. She brightened visibly when Garrett entered the room. Lilah and Bill followed.

"Are you here to bust me out of here? They won't let me leave unless I've got a ride. Dilaudid makes me dizzy."

"Yes, ma'am," Garrett said, doffing an imaginary hat. "Can you take her home, Bill? I've got Lilah and my truck isn't that big."

"You got it."

Lilah sat at the end of Ro's bed, observing the easy friendship between the three coworkers. Ro wouldn't be able to work for at least a week, maybe two. She didn't know anything about the woman, other than her proclivity for tattoos and piercings. Was she on her own? Did she have a family? Would she be able to survive without an income? Garrett would pay her anyway, wouldn't he? And Bill. He wore a wedding ring. Did he have kids? Danny's asshole friends could have ruined all of this. *Danny shoulda messed you up a hell of a lot more than he did.* Hank hadn't returned to Libations just to trash the place. He'd been after Garrett.

"Lilah, darlin'? Bill's going to get the car and I've gotta pay the bill. Can you help Ro get dressed? I'll be back in a couple minutes." Garrett interrupted her panicked thoughts, squeezing her fingers.

"Uh, okay."

Alone, Lilah helped Ro up. The tiny woman swayed for a second, giggled, then got her footing. "Last time I had Dilaudid, I thought I was flying. Fucking drugs. Pants are on the chair. Grab 'em for me?"

"I'm really sorry, Ro," Lilah whispered. "You got hurt because of me."

"Bullshit. I got hurt because your ex is a fucking loon with friends so stupid they'll break into a bar the night they threaten you in front of a dozen patrons. I'm just glad Garrett wasn't there. The big one—the one who attacked you?—he wanted to rip Garrett's leg off and beat him over the head with it. Stupid fucker. Grabbed me and threw me against the bar. He was headed for the back office. Thought Garrett was there. Bill shocked the hell out of him."

Images of Garrett, bloodied, lying dead on the floor without his prosthetic raced through her mind. They were still out there. Sure, the police knew their names, but would they find them before they found Garrett? Or her?

"Tell him I'm sorry," she said and raced out of the room. She ignored Ro's call behind her. How she managed to slip past Garrett, she never knew, but she found herself outside the hospital alone. A moment of fiddling with her phone and the call connected. "I need a cab. I'm at Swedish Medical Center. Can you hurry?"

"We have someone a few blocks away, ma'am."

"Good." Memories, fears, and dreams warred in her mind. She'd been happy these past few weeks. Happier than she thought possible. But that was over now. She couldn't stay. If she stayed, sooner or later, Garrett would end up hurt.

The yellow cab pulled up as Garrett called her name from somewhere behind her. "Lilah, wait!"

"I'm sorry," she sobbed, diving into the back seat. "Drive. Please. Kenmore. University and Grand."

Garrett's fingers scraped against the door a second too late. "Lilah!"

~

"Fuck," he growled as the cab pulled away.

Ro cleared her throat. "Garrett? I screwed up."

"Explain." He turned, softening slightly. Ro leaned heavily against Bill. She was wrapped in his coat.

"I ramble when I'm on pain meds. I may have told her that Hank was after you tonight."

"Goddammit. She was already blaming herself for your injuries, the bar. That fucking bastard screwed with her for years. How in the hell am I supposed to fix this?" He pulled out his phone and called her. After three rings, the call went to voicemail. A moment later, she texted him.

I can't see you any more. It's better this way. Safer. I'm sorry.

"Hell, no," he muttered, then typed a reply. *I'm not losing you over some fuckwit mouthbreather who's too stupid to realize my cameras caught everything and he's going to spend serious time in jail. Please talk to me.*

Goodbye, Garrett.

"Goddamn fucking asshole. We're going to have words."

"If you're talking about that asshole who took me down, get in line," Ro said. "As soon as I can move my arm again, I want a go at him."

Garrett enveloped her in a gentle hug. "No, you don't. You'll go home and rest. Do you need someone to stay with you? I could call one of the servers."

"Pish," she said, the silly dismissal making Garrett chuckle despite his worry for Lilah. "I've been taking care of myself since I was fourteen and ran away from home. I got this. As long as I don't have to drive till the meds wear off, I'm good."

Bill withdrew his keys and shook them. "I'll take you home. Boss, I'm assuming you're going to need me tomorrow. Uh, today."

"I'm going to need you all week. I was supposed to be off tomorrow night with Lilah in Portland. She's politely informed me that we're through, but I'm not lettin' her go without a fight. If her ex Brogan has other friends, I'm worried for her safety."

"The only day I'm booked is Thursday. It's my cousin's baby shower."

Garrett got in his truck, determined to talk to Lilah if it killed him. He was tired enough that he worried it would.

~

"Lilah, open up. Please." He banged on the door, cringing at the sound. He hoped none of her neighbors complained.

"Go away, Garrett. It was fun while it lasted, but it's over now."

Even through the door Garrett could tell that Lilah was crying. If he didn't think he'd scare the crap out of her, he'd have broken down her door. The idea that she was sad or scared inside that tiny apartment where he couldn't get to her killed him. He'd thought rehab had been the hardest thing he'd ever done. No. Rehab had nothing on this moment. "Ro's going to be fine."

"Go home. Go back to your life without me."

"I don't want a life without you, Lilah. Can't you see that?"

Silence met his words. He pressed his ear to the door, catching the sobs and her ragged breathing. She must be sitting on the floor, close enough to touch him if it weren't for the damn door.

"If you're going to end things, you're going to do it face-to-face. You owe me that much." It was a risk he had to take.

Two locks snicked and the door opened a crack. She didn't even release the chain. Her tear-stained face bore the stress he felt, magnified tenfold. Tissues littered what little of the floor he could see. The dark circles around her eyes had turned red and puffy with her tears.

He softened his voice, unclenched his hands, and slumped a little so he wouldn't appear so intimidating. "Fuck, darlin'. I'd never hurt you. You know that, right? For the love of God, please tell me you know."

She didn't answer.

"Lilah, don't do this to me. To us. We have something special. I lo—"

"Don't. Don't say it."

"Goddammit. I will say it. I love you, Lilah. I want to be with you." Garrett reached out, but she shrunk back. The door slammed in his face.

"Lilah!"

A door opened at the end of the hall. "Keep it down or I'm calling the cops!"

"Sorry," Garrett said, shoving his hands into his pockets. He wasn't going to get her to listen this way. All he'd do was scare her. He had to find another way.

chapter ten

Lilah took a bath, figuring that her tears wouldn't make such a mess if she was surrounded by water. She missed Garrett. He'd called and texted a dozen times over the past two days. He'd never pressed, never yelled, but he'd begged and pleaded with her to let him come over or meet him somewhere—anywhere. She had to go to work in the morning and she hoped to all that was holy that he wouldn't be waiting for her when she stepped outside her apartment. Thoughts of Danny consumed her. "He's not Danny. He won't ambush you," she told herself. Maybe she'd go in early. Very early. Or not at all. She could call in sick. *No, not the day after a promotion. You have to go.*

Dr. Lefterts had talked her through the worst of the hours, the ones when Lilah had wanted to run away for good. She'd even packed a bag: her laptop, a few of her favorite outfits, the first copy of her book, and a photo of her parents. She figured she could start over somewhere cheaper. The Midwest maybe. Though she loved Seattle. This was her home—had been from the first time she'd visited the city in college. But though the doctor had encouraged her to talk to Garrett, that was the one thing she couldn't do.

"I don't want him to see me like this. He deserves someone who isn't broken."

"Everyone is broken, Lilah. We've talked about this many times. You were happy with him, yes?"

Lilah sniffled and wiped at her swollen eyes. "Happier than I thought possible. He understood me. I never felt like I was less than his equal."

"And he said he loves you."

"He can't. Even if he did, he won't now. I put him in danger. Then I pushed him away."

Dr. Lefterts clucked her tongue. "Lilah, did it ever occur to you that you did what you always feared a man would do to you? By not even talking to him, you've taken his choices away. Maybe he does love you. There are good men out there. Great ones even. What if he's one of them? Maybe he's not, but until you talk to him, you're never going to find out."

Lilah didn't have a response to that. Not a good one. Dr. Lefterts was right, but that didn't make it any easier. She could let Garrett in and possibly lose him to one of Danny's asshole friends, or she could keep him out, run away, and lose the possibility of something wonderful. But it'd hurt less if she walked away, wouldn't it?

"Don't run, Lilah. Give yourself a week, maybe two, before you see him. But at least call him on the phone. Or respond to his text messages. Ignoring him isn't going to do anyone any good."

"I won't run away. But I'm not ready to talk to him either. Maybe tomorrow." *Or never*.

She watched sappy movies on Netflix, wrote more than ten thousand words on a new story about lost love and heartache, did enough crunches and yoga to leave her spent, and still she cried. Falling into bed Sunday night, she picked up her phone. Four more texts and her voicemail was full. She played the last message.

"Lilah, I know you're screenin' your calls, but maybe you won't delete this without givin' it a listen. Hank and his brother Larry are in jail. I don't know if Danny put them up to it or not, but I'm goin' to find out. You've made it pretty clear you don't want to see me, so I'm givin' up. For now. I love you and I don't see that changin' any time soon, but you don't have to worry about me breakin' down your door or harassin' your phone. You know where to find me."

She played his message four times just to hear the sound of his voice and eventually cried herself to sleep.

Between the weekend and the lack of organization in the police department, it had taken Garrett four days to track down Danny Brogan. He'd been sent down to Mason County, a facility for sex offenders and domestic violence perpetrators. It was the last place Garrett wanted to go, but if he didn't get some answers, he wasn't sure Lilah would ever trust anyone again. Ro, back at work after only a single night off, was manning Libations for him. She couldn't make any drinks that required the use of the shaker, but she could pour his custom shrubs, wine, and beer. Bill picked up the slack, and there hadn't been any more trouble. Still, Garrett wouldn't rest easy until he talked to Brogan.

He had to wait until Friday for visiting day, but after a dozen calls to Brogan's lawyer and Garrett's own, he got his name on the right list. The drive took him almost two hours, and by the time he parked, his right leg ached.

It had done that all week. The stress of being without Lilah wasn't helping. He couldn't sleep and existed on a toxic mix of caffeine, scotch, protein shakes, and the bar's nuts and olives. He spent every morning pushing his body to the limit at the gym, took a nap at noon to ease the exhaustion, and then he'd head to the bar at three, where Ro would try and usually fail to get him to eat something healthy. He'd work until midnight and then head home to do it all over again the next day.

He limped into the jail, got his ID badge, and took a seat at one of the tiny chipped, scratched tables that filled the room. There were a handful of others, inmates dressed in gray, visitors in various bright colors. Quiet conversations provided dull background noise for Garrett's thudding heartbeat. He needed to know if Brogan was behind the attack. Hank and his brother weren't talking yet, and Lilah wasn't safe if there were more of Brogan's buddies out there, hell-bent on revenge.

A door opened and a guard directed Danny to Garrett's table. The man had changed. He'd been largely out of shape when he'd tried to kill Lilah. Now he had packed on fifty pounds of solid muscle. A scar bisected his right cheek and his knuckles were marked with crude prison tattoos. Garrett fought to tear his gaze away from the effects of imprisonment to look Brogan in the eyes.

"What the fuck are you doing here?" Brogan asked. "You're fucking my girl. Aren't you?"

"Sit down," Garrett growled. "Now. And she's definitely *not* your girl."

"We'll see about that."

"One of your cronies attacked Lilah the other night. Came after me a few hours later. You know anything about that?"

Brogan took a step forward, puffed out his chest, and took a seat. His hands lay flat on the table. Something in those dark blue eyes confirmed Garrett's suspicions.

"You do. Fucking piece of shit. I'd kill you right here if I thought I could get away with it. They caught Hank last night. Along with his Neanderthal halfwit brother. I'm headed to the police station this afternoon. I'd say you've got all of a day, maybe two, before they charge you. Accessory to property damage, breaking and entering, assault and battery. Hank hit Lilah a few hours before he tried to trash my bar and he hurt my bartender. There are records, you know. Your phone calls are all monitored in prison, shithead. Hank isn't the smartest tool in the shed. Neither are you for that matter. How many of your asshole friends did you talk to? Because I'll find them all. Or rather, the police will. You're goin' to be in here for a very long time once they all roll over on you."

Danny lunged. He tackled Garrett in the chair, and sent him toppling to the floor. He landed a couple of hard punches to Garrett's ribs and kneed him in the groin. A guard raced over and grabbed Danny under the arms. The pressure on Garrett's torso lifted, but Danny kicked out, catching Garrett's bad leg half a dozen times before a second guard cuffed Danny and dragged him from the room. Pain shot up Garrett's back, down through his leg. He didn't care. He'd endure the beating a dozen more times if it ensured Danny Boyle never bothered Lilah again.

"Sir? Are you okay?" A tall guard stood over him, offering him a hand.

"Yeah. My leg's out of whack. Is there somewhere private I can go to fix it?"

"Fix it?" The guard's eyes widened.

"Prosthetic. Mid-thigh. I need to drop my pants, reattach it securely."

The guard helped him up. Garrett held onto his thigh with one hand and threw the other arm around the guard's shoulders. In a back office, he took off his jeans, readjusted, and tightened the mechanism that held his leg in place. He had to get home. His stump was going to swell up pretty quickly and he'd be unable to walk comfortably. He needed ice, some elevation, and a good night's sleep. Maybe two. At least he could rest now. Danny would get a hell of a lot more time added to his sentence and the cops would investigate all of his phone calls—and hopefully find anyone else who may be a danger to Lilah.

"You want to press charges, sir?"

"You're damn right I do. Point me to your warden."

Garrett limped down to the warden's office, met with officers from the local precinct, and gave a detailed statement. He didn't make it home until close to nine p.m. and opted for the elevator as opposed to the stairs. He stumbled into his apartment and collapsed on his bed. He didn't even have it in him to get the ice. Stripping, he grimaced. Three purple bruises darkened his ribs. His leg was red and swollen all the way up to his hip. Another two foot-sized bruises on his outer thigh would make wearing his prosthetic damn near impossible tomorrow. He pulled out his phone to document the damage to his body. The police would want evidence.

It was Friday night. Two days before Valentine's Day. Days ago, before this trouble, he'd planned to take Lilah out for a steak dinner and give her a key to his apartment, a step towards commitment for both of them. Now he wondered if he'd ever see her again. One last text message. He couldn't keep pining over her forever. He'd done all he could and this would have to be the end.

Brogan set Hank on you. Us. Had to prove it so I went to see him. It's over now. Warden thinks he'll double his sentence. Maybe more. No one's going to hurt you again.

A few minutes later, as he was drifting towards sleep, his phone dinged.

You went to see him?

Garrett thumbed out a quick reply. *Had to do something. He's going down for conspiracy to commit assault, breaking and entering. Among other charges. Please call me. I need to hear your voice.*

He must have sounded appropriately desperate, because Lilah called him five minutes later.

"Garrett?" The pain in her voice broke him.

"Lilah, it's been killin' me not seein' you. You don't have to be scared any more. Let me come over. Please." He didn't want to leave his bed—wasn't sure he could—but he'd do anything to see her.

"I can't," she whispered.

He fisted his hands in the sheets. That wasn't an answer. "Why not? Did I do something? If I did, tell me so I can never do it again." He tried to sit up, grunted from the pain, and collapsed back down again.

"Are you okay?" she asked.

"It's nothin'. Please answer my question."

"You've never done anything but be perfect. I'm the one who's screwed up. I shouldn't have called. Nothing hurts me as much as saying goodbye to you, but I have to do it. You'll be better off without me. Find someone who makes you happy."

"You make me happy, darlin'. You're the one for me."

"I . . . I think I loved you, Garrett."

The click of her hanging up was the final nail through his heart.

~

Libations was hopping the next night when Lilah pulled open the door. She'd been prepared to never see Garrett again, but her lawyer had called that morning, filled in all of the details about Garrett's visit with Danny, along with the warden's belief that Danny's sentence should be extended to ten years. That, coupled with a cryptic message from Ro blaming her for Garrett's injuries—what injuries?—and she had to see him.

She'd worn a dress, a modest black number that hugged her hips and dipped slightly over her breasts. She hadn't done it to impress him. It had been the first thing she'd found in her closet. Hadn't it been? So what if she did her makeup, brushed her hair until it shined, and painted her nails. It wasn't for him. It was for her. So she could feel confident.

Ro was at the bar. She moved slowly, but her smile for her customers was genuine. At least some things hadn't changed. Garrett was nowhere to be seen. Was he even here? Lilah squeezed between several obvious dates to snag the only stool left and waited for Ro to notice her. The bartender's hazel eyes narrowed and she stalked over to Lilah with fists clenched. Lilah shrank back a bit, looking to either side of her to see if anyone might come to her aid.

"What the hell are you doing here?" she asked. "And dressed like that? Trying to rub it in his face? He's gone through hell this week for you. Which you'd know if you bothered to take any of his calls."

"Please. I need to know he's okay. My lawyer told me what he did with Danny. How badly is he hurt?" She leaned forward, risking Ro's wrath. The truth of it hit her over the head. She'd denied it for a week, made herself miserable, made *him* miserable. It had to end. "I . . . I love him, Ro. I want—no I need—to fix this."

Ro made a sound that might have been a *harrumph*, set a glass down in front of Lilah, and poured her a generous shot of scotch. "Drink up, chickie. He's at home, but you and I are going to have a little talk before you go see him. Because he's been fucking miserable without you and I'm tired of it."

The cab dropped her off at Garrett's building a little after eleven. Ro paid in advance, and told the driver that if he didn't drop Lilah off at the building, she'd yank his balls out his throat. She'd known the man, or so Lilah hoped, because that didn't seem like a smart thing to say to a cab driver who could drop you off in a dark alley in the middle of Tacoma if he felt like it. On her own, scared out of her mind that she'd waited too long, she climbed the steps to Garrett's fourth-floor apartment. Wind whipped her hair around her face and pelted her coat with tiny icy droplets. It was supposed to snow tonight, Seattle's first snowstorm for the year.

Three short raps on his door and her heart leapt into her throat. She wasn't prepared for the sight that greeted her.

Garrett threw open the door, balancing on his crutches, wearing nothing but a pair of pajama pants with the right leg hemmed short. Bruises covered his torso, purple and blue and red against the tattoos. His hair was damp, and a few drops of water dotted his chest and his arms. She caught the scent of his soap: cedar, sandalwood, and a hint of pine. The steam from what had obviously been his shower wafted out the door.

"Hi." It was all she could manage.

"Lilah." His voice was hard, perhaps harder than his chiseled face. He didn't say her name with the reverence he'd always carried. It wasn't a prayer, it was a curse. A step towards him was met with a flinch and he turned, making his way awkwardly into his living room. "It's goin' to snow. Mind not heatin' the whole city? Either come in and talk or run away again. But close the goddamn door."

It was her turn to flinch. He'd never been anything but caring and sweet with her, even when he was angry. This Garrett—this one was beyond angry. She had to fix this. Two steps and she was inside. She shut the door firmly behind her. A cardboard box at her feet held her toothbrush, two neatly folded pairs of underwear, a sleep shirt, a pair of fleece pants, and a pair of her socks. Before she'd bolted, they'd been sleeping together four nights a week. Mondays and Thursdays at her place, Fridays and Saturdays at his. His stuff was still in her dresser, on her nightstand, and her pair of crutches from her broken leg was under *his* side of the bed. It struck her then that she'd never truly wanted to leave him. She'd been so stupid.

"If you've got somethin' to say . . . " He lowered himself down with a stifled grunt and rested his crutches next to him. He pulled a T-shirt from the back of the couch and tugged it over his head.

"I'm sorry."

"That's not enough, darlin'. It would have been, a week ago. Hell, two days ago. Not after last night. You broke me, Lilah. I didn't think I could be that low again, but you did it with five words."

"I think I loved you." She looked down, her lower lip wobbling.

"That would be them. Why the hell are you here? I told you last night, you're free of him and his buddies. I talked to the warden. He's goin' to solitary for a long time for attackin' me in the visitor's center. When he gets outta solitary, he's goin' to be monitored. Heavily. I suppose he could get paroled in ten years or so, but a fuckwit like him'll do something else stupid before that happens."

Lilah took another step forward. Garrett's hard gaze urged her—dared her—to turn back. "I went to the bar. Ro . . . I'm not welcome there any more. Not unless I fix this."

"She's lookin' out for me. You want to go on Mondays when I'm off, enjoy. But don't come in when I'm there."

A tear trailed down her cheek and she dashed it away. "Do you want me to beg? To get down on my knees and tell you how sorry I am? I freaked out. Badly. I ran, because running is easier than dealing with my feelings for you. I haven't had—been allowed—feelings in a long time and sometimes, they get so bottled up that they terrify me. I've been with four men in my entire life. Four! Two in college, Danny, and you. I'm twenty-nine-years-old and I've never been in love." She took the final step and knelt in front of him, her hands smoothing up his thighs. He flinched. "Until now."

"What did you say?" He sat up with a grunt, narrowing his eyes at her. Heat from his body seeped into her fingers.

"I know why I was so scared this week. Yes, it was Danny and his dumbass friends. But that was only the catalyst. I ran . . . I gave in to the fear and ran . . . because I *love* you. Because I couldn't stand the idea that anyone could ever hurt you because of me."

She had so much more to say, but Garrett didn't give her the chance. He reached for her, dragged her onto his lap, and smoothed a callused hand over her cheek. "Say it again."

"I love you."

"And what are you going to do about it?" The final dare. The only one that mattered.

"Stay. If you'll have me."

His kiss was all the answer she needed.

epilogue

THE SNOWSTORM HIT with a vengeance that Seattle hadn't seen in ten years. Buses weren't running, ice covered the roads, and only the snowplows could really get around. As Seattle only had three of them, no one was going anywhere fast. Lilah didn't care. She'd woken up in Garrett's bed. On Valentine's Day.

She'd been unprepared for the tenderness he'd shown the previous night. He had a couple of bruised ribs and his leg was red and swollen. He didn't think he'd be able to wear his prosthetic for another couple of days. She'd already called in to work telling them she wouldn't be in the next day. She planned to spend the next two days with Garrett to reclaim what her fear had taken from them.

Lilah didn't know if they were back on solid ground yet, but he'd held her all night, told her he loved her more than once. Naked, she stretched under the blankets. A card rustled and fluttered to the floor. The red envelope with the silver embossed heart brought a smile to her face and she tore into it. The outside of the card was simple: another silver heart pierced with an arrow.

Happy Valentine's Day

Inside, it was blank save for Garrett's words.

Your dreams matter. You matter. Always.

He remembered her mantra. "Garrett?"

"In the kitchen, darlin'."

"I'm wearing one of your shirts." She rummaged through his top drawer, finding a long-sleeved Shade's Whiskey Station T-shirt. It was a dress on her but she didn't care. She'd live in Garrett's clothes until she had to go home again. Scents of coffee and butter made her stomach growl. Garrett stood at the stove, balanced on crutches while tending to something in a pan.

"I didn't hear you get up."

He turned. The intensity of his stare stopped her in her tracks. "You were tired."

"I don't think I've slept a full night since . . . "

"Since you freaked out on me."

She blushed. "Yeah."

"Me either. Sit down. I want to talk to you."

After a quick detour to her box of things by the door for underwear, pants, and socks, she took a seat on the couch. "I don't get coffee first?" Nerves had her fingers shaking. Maybe he hadn't forgiven her.

"It'll wait. This won't."

"You're scaring me."

Garrett turned off the stove and put a lid on the pan. He swung his way over to her, set aside his crutches, and hopped a couple of times, collapsing next to her. "I hate those sticks." He rubbed his right leg, wincing. "I'm not sure I've ever been happier for snow. At least I don't have to work. I've already decided we're not openin' today. We'll lose out on the Valentine's Day crowd—whoever's stupid enough to go out in this weather—but I won't have any of my people drivin' when the roads are like this."

"Garrett?" Her voice cracked. She couldn't take much more.

He chuckled and wrapped his arms around her. "Relax, darlin'. You look like I'm about to take your puppy away."

"I hurt you. And you forgave me, so quickly. Or I thought you did . . . "

"I don't hold grudges, Lilah. That's not me. But I do feel like we've got somethin' else to discuss. Somethin' important."

"What?" She was close enough she feared Garrett could smell her morning breath. She pulled away, drawing her knees up to her chest and wrapping her arms around them.

"We're together now. I'm not lettin' anythin' come between us again. But a relationship is a two-way street. We both need to put the work in—figure out how to make each other happy. So I'm askin' you for somethin'."

"What?" She was so relieved that he wasn't kicking her out that she'd agree to anything.

He tangled their fingers, staring down at the tattoo on her wrist. "If you ever want to run again, you talk to me. Face to face. Not through a goddamn door. You'll let me hold you. If you still feel like turnin' tail after that, fine. But not before we talk. It's the only thing I'll ask you. My only demand. Promise me."

Lilah nodded. She could do that. "I promise."

"There's one more thing. But this isn't something I'm askin'. It's something I'm givin'." He dipped a hand into his pocket and withdrew a silver key with a red ribbon threaded through the top. "Maybe, if you think you can, you could bring some clothes over. I've got some space in my closet. A drawer. A shelf in the medicine cabinet."

"You want me to . . . "

"I *want* you to move in with me. But I'll settle for this. For now."

Lilah took the key from his palm. It was warm. She looked around his apartment. It wasn't much bigger than hers, but it was a home. The photographs on the bookshelves, the television with a messy pile of DVDs off to the side, and the stack of books on the coffee table all spoke of a life lived here. It was a life she wanted to be a part of.

"I need my own space, Garrett. At least for a while. The occasional night on my own, a place I can retreat to when things get too much. I can't promise I won't have more bad days. I *can* promise I won't run. I'll ask for a night apart. Even a few days. But we'll talk. And once we can get to the hardware store, I'll get you a key to my place, if you promise you won't use it on the days I ask for a little space. If I take a little bit of your closet, you could have some of mine."

"I'd like that very much, darlin'. Very much indeed."

"Happy Valentine's Day, Garrett." She straddled him, threaded her fingers through his hair, and leaned down for a quick kiss.

"Yes, it is," he said, pulling her closer. "Happy Valentine's Day, Lilah. I love you."

This time, her name on his lips was more than a prayer. It was a promise.

Thank you for reading Love and Libations. If you enjoyed Garrett and Lilah's story, I hope you'll take a few minutes and leave a review on Amazon and Goodreads. Reviews don't have to be long or complicated. If you'd like to write a novel on why you liked my novel, I'd certainly love that, but even a few words about how the book made you feel would be wonderful.

Reviews are an author's best friend. We live for them. A good review can turn your entire day around. It takes less than a minute to do (unless you're writing that novel, of course) and it can mean so much. If you leave a review, please email me at patricia@pdeddy.com so I can personally thank you. I hope you'll also consider recommending this book to your friends and book clubs.

I hope you'll check out the first book in the Holidays and Heroes series, *Mistletoe and Mochas*. The next book, *Fireworks and Flirtations*, will be out this summer. Sign up for my newsletter so you can be the first to hear about any pre-order or release day news!

a serious note

This story was close to my heart, because I have some personal experience with abusive relationships. No, I was never hit or threatened, but I was worn down over the years by a toxic situation that left me questioning who I was and whether I was worth anything. Some of the phrases used in Love and Libations came directly from my own life.

Domestic violence is a serious issue, but emotional abuse is the infrequently mentioned little sister that I wanted to bring to light with this story. Emotional abusers do many of the same things as physical abusers, but since they never hit, shake, or slap them, the victim doesn't always realize that they're being abused until it's too late. Emotional abusers cut their victims off from friends, make them feel worthless, and generally dismiss them. Often, the digs are so mild that the victim doesn't even realize it until they've been so worn down, they can't get out.

If you or a loved one is the victim of domestic violence or emotional abuse, please talk to someone. There are a few resources I've compiled that I can recommend. Each of these comes from a person who has actively used their services.

Safe Horizon
safehorizon.org

Refuge
refuge.org.uk

New Beginnings
newbegin.org

The other links I hope you'll check out are those for organizations that help wounded veterans. Again, these links were compiled from personal recommendations I received from veterans or friends of veterans who used these organizations.

Wounded Warrior Project
woundedwarriorproject.org

Vet Sports
vetsports.org

books by patricia d. eddy

Do you love Urban Fantasy? Check out *A Shift in the Water*, my bestselling tale of werewolves and elementals.

Do you love Paranormal Romance? I have two Paranormal Romance series available now!

By the Fates

By the Fates, Freed
Destined, a By the Fates Story
By the Fates, Fought

In Blood

Secrets in Blood
Revelations in Blood (coming soon)

Newsletter: http://eepurl.com/CXPOj
Facebook: http://www.facebook.com/pdeddy.author
Twitter: http://www.twitter.com/patricia_eddy
Pinterest: http://www.pinterest.com/patriciadeddy
Website: http://www.pdeddy.com

acknowledgements

WRITING IS ONE of the most solitary hobbies one can choose. Publishing, however, is anything but solitary. This book would not be what it is without the love, support, and assistance of some wonderful people in my life.

My friends who encouraged me to take on this sensitive and hard subject, thank you. You gave me the courage to tell a bit of my own story through Lilah and her words, and heal. Thank you for being patient when I was a bit of a mess, when I stressed out over deadlines, and when I wondered if I was doing the right thing at all. Your words of encouragement, advice, and patience was sorely needed.

My wonderful and talented business partner and marketing manager, Samantha. In a year, you've become someone I rely on, of course, but you are so much more. You are a dear friend, a confidant, and a co-conspirator. I can't wait to see what the future has in store for PageCurl and for us individually. I know it's going to rock. We will take over the world, but not in a lunatic overlord sort of way because that doesn't sound fun for everyone else.

I wouldn't be where I am without you and whatever I did in some past life to harness enough good luck to meet you, well, it must have been epic.

Indie authors, you won't find a better assistant and marketing manager. You can find Samantha and her amazing writing at skwills.com or hire her as your own book manager and marketing genius at pagecurl.net. Oh, and if you like romance, you should check out her debut novel, *Starting from Lost*.

Another benefit of meeting Samantha was that I got to meet Melody Barber, my cover designer for this book. Melody is so easy to work with. She's fast and approachable and all I have to do is give her a couple of ideas and she's off running. I love everything about this cover and hope you do too. You can find Melody at bookcoversbymelody.wordpress.com.

I used Clare C. Marshall for editing and formatting. We've had a long road together, Clare and I. She saw my writing when it was at its worst—before I released *By the Fates, Freed*. She's been patient and kind, helpful and encouraging. I want to thank her for helping me polish one of the most personal books I've ever written.

Lastly, to my readers. Thank you for reading, for sending notes, leaving reviews, and buying my books. I couldn't do this without you (or at least, I couldn't be successful at it). Thank you from the bottom of my heart.

drink recipes

Garrett shared several of his drink recipes with me and I wanted to share them with you. I hope you enjoy them.

Seattle's Long Wet Kiss

- *1 oz bourbon*
- *1 oz peach liqueur*
- *Lemon sage bitters*
- *Splash grenadine*

Mix the bourbon, peach liqueur, and lemon-sage bitters in a cocktail shaker with ice. Shake well. Strain into a rocks glass with or without ice and top with a splash of grenadine.

Naughty Toddy

- *1.5 oz bourbon*
- *1/2 oz mead*
- *1/2 oz pepper vodka*
- *Black gunpowder tea*
- *Mist of absinthe*

Mist the glass with the absinthe. Brew tea according to your preferences. Mix in the bourbon, mead, and pepper vodka. Finish with another mist of absinthe.

Garrett's Hot Toddy

- *1.5 oz bourbon*
- *1/2 oz mead*
- *1 oz peach liqueur*
- *Chamomile tea*
- *Mist of ginger liqueur*

Mist the glass with the ginger liqueur. Brew tea according to your preferences. Mix in the bourbon, mead, and peach liqueur. Finish with another mist of absinthe.